THE OCEANS OF VENUS

The Oceans of Venus

Isaac Asimov

NEW ENGLISH LIBRARY
TIMES MIRROR

First published in the USA by Doubleday & Co. Inc., 1954
Published in Great Britain by New English Library Ltd., 1973
Foreword Copyright © 1972 by Isaac Asimov

∗

FIRST NEL PAPERBACK EDITION AUGUST 1974

∗

NEL Books are published by
New English Library Limited from Barnard's Inn, Holborn, London, E.C.1.
Printed in Finland by Uusi Kivipaino Oy.

450 01926 8

Dedication

CONTENTS

FOREWORD

THIS BOOK WAS FIRST PUBLISHED IN 1954, and the description of the surface of Venus was in accordance with astronomic beliefs of the period.

Since 1954, however, astronomical knowledge of the inner Solar system has advanced enormously because of the use of radar beams and rockets.

In the late 1950s, the quantity of radio waves received from Venus made it seem that the surface of Venus might be much hotter than had been thought. On August 27, 1962, a rocket probe called "Mariner II" was launched in the direction of Venus. It skimmed by within 21,000 miles of Venus on December 14, 1962. Measuring the radio waves emitted by the planet, it turned out that the surface temperature everywhere was indeed considerably higher than the boiling point of water.

This meant that far from having a worldwide ocean, as described in this book, Venus had no ocean at all. All of Venus's water is in the form of water vapor in its clouds, and the surface is exceedingly hot and is bonedry. The atmosphere of Venus is, moreover, denser than had been thought and is almost entirely carbon dioxide.

Nor had it been known, in 1954, how long it took Venus to rotate on its axis. In 1964, radar beams bounced off Venus's surface showed that it was turning once in every 243 days (eighteen days longer than its year) and in the "wrong" direction as compared with other planets.

I hope that the readers enjoy this story anyway, but I would not wish them to be misguided into accepting as fact some of the material which was "accurate" in 1954 but which is now outdated.

ISAAC ASIMOV
November, 1970

Chapter 1

THROUGH THE CLOUDS OF VENUS

LUCKY STARR AND JOHN BIGMAN JONES kicked themselves up from the gravity-free Space Station No. 2 and drifted toward the planetary coaster that waited for them with its air lock open. Their movements had the grace of long practice under non-gravity conditions, despite the fact that their bodies seemed thick and grotesque in the space suits they wore.

Bigman arched his back as he moved upward and craned his head to stare once again at Venus. His voice sounded loudly in Lucky's ear through the suit's radio. "Space! Look at that rock, will you?" Every inch of Bigman's five-foot-two was tense with the thrill of the sight.

Bigman had been born and bred on Mars and had never in his life been so close to Venus. He was used to ruddy planets and rocky asteroids. He had even visited green and blue Earth. But here, now, was something that was pure gray and white.

Venus filled over half the sky. It was only two thousand miles away from the space station they were on. Another space station was on the opposite side of the planet. These two stations, acting as receiving depots for Venus-bound spaceships, streaked about the planet in a three-hour period of revolution, following one another's tracks like little puppies forever chasing their tails.

Yet from those space stations, close though they were

to Venus, nothing could be seen of the planet's surface. No continents showed, no oceans, no deserts or mountains, no green valleys. Whiteness, only brilliant whiteness, interspersed with shifting lines of gray.

The whiteness was the turbulent cloud layer that hovered eternally over all of Venus, and the gray lines marked the boundaries where cloud masses met and clashed. Vapor moved downward at those boundaries, and below those gray lines, on Venus's invisible surface, it rained.

Lucky Starr said, "No use looking at Venus, Bigman. You'll be seeing plenty of it, close up, for a while. It's the sun you ought to be saying good-by to."

Bigman snorted. To his Mars-accustomed eyes, even Earth's sun seemed swollen and overbright. The sun, as seen from Venus's orbit, was a bloated monster. It was two and a quarter times as bright as Earth's sun, four times as bright as the familiar sun on Bigman's Mars. Personally, he was glad that Venus's clouds would hide its sun. He was glad that the space station always arranged its vanes in such a way as to block off the sunlight.

Lucky Starr said, "Well, you crazy Martian, are you getting in?"

Bigman had brought himself to a halt at the lip of the open lock by the casual pressure of one hand. He was still looking at Venus. The visible half was in the full glare of the sun, but at the eastern side the night shadow was creeping in, moving quickly as the space station raced on in its orbit.

Lucky, still moving upward, caught the lip of the lock in his turn and brought his other space-suited hand flat against Bigman's seat. Under the gravity-free conditions, Bigman's little body went tumbling slowly inward, while Lucky's figure bobbed outward.

Lucky's arm muscle contracted, and he floated up and inward with an easy, flowing motion. Lucky had no cause for a light heart at the moment, but he was forced into a smile when he found Bigman spread-eagled in mid-air, with the tip of one gauntleted finger against the inner lock holding him steady. The outer lock closed as Lucky passed through.

Bigman said, "Listen, you wombug, someday I'm walking out on you and you can get yourself another——"

Air hissed into the small room, and the inner lock opened. Two men floated rapidly through, dodging Bigman's dangling feet. The one in the lead, a stocky fellow with dark hair and a surprisingly large mustache, said, "Is there any trouble, gentlemen?"

The second man, taller, thinner, and with lighter hair but a mustache just as large, said, "Can we help you?"

Bigman said loftily, "You can help us by giving us room and letting us get our suits off." He had flicked himself to the floor and was removing his suit as he spoke. Lucky had already shucked his.

The men went through the inner lock. It, too, closed behind them. The space suits, their outer surface cold with the cold of space, were frosting over as moisture from the warm air of the coaster congealed upon them. Bigman tossed them out of the coaster's warm, moist air on to the tiled racks, where the ice might melt.

The dark-haired man said, "Let's see, now. You two are William Williams and John Jones. Right?"

Lucky said, "I'm Williams." Using that alias under ordinary conditions was second nature to Lucky by now. It was customary for Council of Science members to shun publicity at all times. It was particularly advisable now with the situation on Venus as confused and uncertain as it was.

Lucky went on, "Our papers are in order, I believe, and our luggage is aboard."

"Everything's all right," the dark-haired one said, "I'm George Reval, pilot, and this is Tor Johnson, my co-pilot. We'll be taking off in a few minutes. If there's anything you want, let us know."

The two passengers were shown to their small cabin, and Lucky sighed inwardly. He was never thoroughly comfortable in space except on his own speed cruiser, the *Shooting Starr,* now at rest in the space station's hangar.

Tor Johnson said in a deep voice, "Let me warn you, by the way, that once we get out of the space station's orbit, we won't be in free fall any more. Gravity will start picking up. If you get space-sick——"

Bigman yelled, "Space-sick! You in-planet goop, I could take gravity changes when I was a baby that you couldn't take right now." He flicked his finger against the wall, turned a slow somersault, touched the wall again, and ended with his feet just a half-inch above the floor. "Try *that* someday when you feel real manly."

"Say," said the co-pilot, grinning, "you squeeze a lot of brash into half a pint, don't you?"

Bigman flushed instantly. "Half a pint! Why, you soup-straining cobber——" he screamed, but Lucky's hand was on his shoulder and he swallowed the rest of the sentence. "See you on Venus," the little Martian muttered darkly.

Tor was still grinning. He followed his chief into the control room toward the head of the ship.

Bigman, his anger gone at once, said to Lucky curiously, "Say, how about those mustaches? Never saw any so big."

Lucky said, "It's just a Venusian custom, Bigman. I think practically everybody grows them on Venus."

"That so?" Bigman fingered his lip, stroking its bareness. "Wonder how I'd look in one."

"With one that big?" smiled Lucky. "It would drown your whole face."

He dodged the punch Bigman threw at him just as the floor trembled lightly beneath their feet and the *Venus Marvel* lifted off the space station. The coaster turned its nose into the contracting spiral trajectory that would carry it "down" to Venus.

Lucky Starr felt the beginnings of a long-overdue relaxation flooding him as the coaster picked up speed. His brown eyes were thoughtful, and his keen, fine-featured face was in repose. He was tall and looked slim, but beneath that deceptive slimness were whip-cord muscles.

Life had already given much to Lucky of both good and evil. He had lost his parents while still a child, lost them in a pirate attack near the very Venus he was now approaching. He had been brought up by his father's dearest friends, Hector Conway, now chief of the Council of Science, and Augustus Henree, section director of the same organization.

Lucky had been educated and trained with but one thought in mind: Someday he was to enter that very Council of Science, whose powers and functions made it the most important and yet least-known body in the galaxy.

It was only a year ago, upon his graduation from the academy, that he had entered into full membership and become dedicated to the advancement of man and the destruction of the enemies of civilization. He was the youngest member of the Council and probably would remain so for years.

Yet already he had won his first battles. On the deserts of Mars and among the dimlit rocks of the asteroid belt, he had met and triumphed over wrong-doing.

But the war against crime and evil is not a short-term conflict, and now it was Venus that was the setting for trouble, a trouble that was particularly disturbing since its details were misty.

Chief of the Council Hector Conway had pinched his lip and said, "I'm not sure whether it's a Sirian conspiracy against the Solar Confederation, or just petty racketeering. Our local men there tend to view it seriously."

Lucky said, "Have you sent any of our trouble shooters?" He was not long back from the asteroids, and he was listening to this with concern.

Conway said, "Yes: Evans."

"Lou Evans?" asked Lucky, his dark eyes lighting with pleasure. "He was one of my roommates at the academy. He's *good*."

"Is he? The Venus office of the Council has requested his removal and investigation on the charge of corruption!"

"*What?*" Lucky was on his feet, horrified. "Uncle Hector, that's impossible."

"Want to go out there and look into it yourself?"

"Do I! Great stars and little asteroids! Bigman and I will take off just as soon as we get the *Shooting Starr* flight-ready."

And now Lucky watched out the porthole thoughtfully, on the last leg of his flight. The night shadow had crept over Venus, and for an hour there was only blackness to be seen. All the stars were hidden by Venus's huge bulk.

Then they were out in the sunlight again, but now the viewport was only gray. They were too close to see the planet as a whole. They were even too close to see the clouds. They were actually inside the cloudy layer.

Bigman, having just finished a large chicken-salad sandwich, wiped his lips and said, "Space, I'd hate to have to pilot a ship through all this muck."

The coaster's wings had snapped out into extended position to take advantage of the atmosphere, and there was a definite difference in the quality of the ship's motion as a result. The buffeting of the winds could be felt and the plunging and lifting of the drafts that sink and rise.

Ships that navigate space are not suitable for the treachery of thick atmosphere. It is for that reason that planets like Earth and Venus, with deep layers of air enshrouding them, require space stations. To those space stations come the ships of deep space. From the stations planetary coasters with retractable wings ride the tricky air currents to the planet's surface.

Bigman, who could pilot a ship from Pluto to Mercury blindfolded, would have been lost at the first thickening wisp of an atmosphere. Even Lucky, who in his intensive training at the academy had piloted coasters, would not have cared to take on the job in the blanketing clouds that surrounded them now.

"Until the first explorers landed on Venus," Lucky said, "all mankind ever saw of the planet was the outer surface of these clouds. They had weird notions about the planet then."

Bigman didn't reply. He was looking into the celloplex container to make sure there wasn't another chicken-salad sandwich hiding there.

Lucky went on. "They couldn't tell how fast Venus was rotating or whether it was rotating at all. They weren't even sure about the composition of Venus's atmosphere. They knew it had carbon dioxide, but until the late 1900s astronomers thought Venus had no water. When ships began to land, mankind found that wasn't so."

He broke off. Despite himself, Lucky's mind returned once again to the coded spacegram he had received in mid-flight, with Earth ten million miles behind. It was from Lou Evans, his old roommate, to whom he had subethered that he was on his way.

The reply was short, blunt, and clear. It was, "Stay away!"

Just that! It was unlike Evans. To Lucky, a message like that meant trouble, big trouble, so he did not "stay away." Instead, he moved the micropile energy output up a notch and increased acceleration to the gasping point.

Bigman was saying, "Gives you a funny feeling, Lucky, when you think that once, long ago, people were all cooped up on Earth. Couldn't get off it no matter what they did. Didn't know anything about Mars or the moon or anywhere. It gives me the shivers."

It was just at that point that they pierced the cloud barrier, and even Lucky's gloomy thoughts vanished at the sight that met their eyes.

It was sudden. One moment they were surrounded by what seemed an eternal milkiness; the next, there was only transparent air about them. Everything below was bathed in a clear, pearly light. Above was the gray undersurface of the clouds.

Bigman said, "Hey, Lucky, look!"

Venus stretched out below them for miles in every direction, and it was a solid carpet of blue-green vegetation. There were no dips or rises in the surface. It was absolutely level, as though it had been planed down by a giant atomic slicer.

Nor was there anything to be seen that would have been normal in an Earthly scene. No roads or houses, no towns or streams. Just blue-green, unvarying, as far as could be seen.

Lucky said, "Carbon dioxide does it. It's the part of the air plants feed on. On Earth there's only three hundredths of one per cent in the air, but here almost ten per cent of the air is carbon dioxide."

Bigman, who had lived for years on the farms of Mars, knew about carbon dioxide. He said, "What makes it so light with all the clouds?"

Lucky smiled. "You're forgetting, Bigman. The sun is over twice as bright here as on earth." Then as he looked out the port again, his smile thinned and vanished.

"Funny," he murmured.

Suddenly, he turned away from the window. "Bigman," he said, "come with me to the pilot room."

In two strides he was out the cabin. In two more, he was at the pilot room. The door wasn't locked. He pulled it open. Both pilots, George Reval and Tor Johnson, were at their places, eyes glued to the controls. Neither turned as they entered.

Lucky said, "Men——"

No response.

He touched Johnson's shoulder, and the co-pilot's arm twitched irritably, shaking off Lucky's grip.

The young Councilman seized Johnson by either shoulder and called, "Get the other one, Bigman!"

The little fellow was already at work on that very job, asking no questions, attacking with a bantam's fury.

Lucky hurled Johnson from him. Johnson staggered back, righted himself, and charged forward. Lucky ducked a wild blow and brought a straight-armed right to the side of the other's jaw. Johnson went down, cold. At nearly the same moment, Bigman, with a quick and skillful twist of George Reval's arm, flung him along the floor and knocked him breathless.

Bigman dragged both pilots outside the pilot room and closed the door on them. He came back to find Lucky handling the controls feverishly.

Only then did he ask for an explanation. "What happened?"

"We weren't leveling off," said Lucky grimly. "I watched the surface, and it was coming up too fast. It still is."

He strove desperately to find the particular control for the ailerons, those vanes that controlled the angle of flight. The blue surface of Venus was much closer. It was rushing at them.

Lucky's eyes were on the pressure gauge. It measured the weight of air above them. The higher it rose, the closer they were to the surface. It was climbing less quickly now. Lucky's fist closed more tightly on the duorod, squeezing the forks together. That must be it. He dared not exert force too rapidly or the ailerons might be whipped off altogether by the screaming gale that flung itself past their ship. Yet there was only five hundred feet to spare before zero altitude.

His nostrils flaring, the cords in his neck standing out, Lucky played those ailerons against the wind.

"We're leveling," breathed Bigman. "We're leveling——"

But there wasn't room enough. The blue-green came up and up till it filled all the view in the port. Then, with a speed that was too great and an angle that was also too great, the *Venus Marvel,* carrying Lucky Starr and Bigman Jones, struck the surface of the planet Venus.

Chapter 2

UNDER THE SEA DOME

HAD THE SURFACE OF VENUS been what it seemed to be at first glance, the *Venus Marvel* would have smashed to scrap and burned to ash. The career of Lucky Starr would have ended at that moment.

Fortunately, the vegetation that had so thickly met the eye was neither grass nor shrubbery, but seaweed. The flat plain was no surface of soil and rock, but water, the top of an ocean that surrounded and covered all of Venus.

The *Venus Marvel*, even so, hit the ocean with a thunderous rattle, tore through the ropy weeds, and boiled its way into the depths. Lucky and Bigman were hurled against the walls.

An ordinary vessel might have been smashed, but the *Venus Marvel* had been designed for entering water at high speed. Its seams were tight; its form, streamlined. Its wings, which Lucky had neither time nor knowledge to retract, were torn loose, and its frame groaned under the shock, but it remained seaworthy.

Down, down it went into the green-black murk of the Venusian ocean. The cloud-diffused light from above was almost totally stopped by the tight weed cover. The ship's artificial lighting did not go on, its workings apparently put out of order by the shock of contact.

Lucky's senses were whirling. "Bigman," he called.

There was no answer, and he stretched out his arms, feeling. His hand touched Bigman's face.

"Bigman!" he called again. He felt the little Martian's chest, and the heart was beating regularly. Relief washed over Lucky.

He had no way of telling what was happening to the ship. He knew he could never find any way of controlling it in the complete darkness that enveloped them. He could only hope that the friction of the water would halt the ship before it struck bottom.

He felt for the pencil flash in his shirt pocket—a little plastic rod some six inches long that, on activation by thumb pressure, became a solid glow of light that streamed out forward, its beam broadening without seeming to weaken appreciably.

Lucky groped for Bigman again and examined him gently. There was a lump on the Martian's temple, but no broken bones so far as Lucky could tell.

Bigman's eyes fluttered. He groaned.

Lucky whispered, "Take it easy, Bigman. We'll be all right." He was far from sure of that as he stepped out into the corridor. The pilots would have to be alive and cooperative if the ship were ever to see home port again.

They were sitting up, blinking at Lucky's flash as he came through the door.

"What happened?" groaned Johnson. "One minute I was at the controls, and then——" There was no hostility, only pain and confusion, in his eyes.

The *Venus Marvel* was back to partial normality. It was limping badly, but its searchlights, fore and aft, had been restored to operation and the emergency batteries had been rigged up to supply them with all the power they would need for vital operations. The churning of the propeller could be dimly heard, and the planetary coaster was displaying, adequately enough, its third function. It was a vessel that could navigate, not only in space and in air, but under water as well.

George Reval stepped into the control room. He was downcast and obviously embarrassed. He had a gash on his cheek, which Lucky had washed, disinfected, and neatly sprayed with koagulum.

Reval said, "There are a few minor seepages, but I plugged them. The wings are gone, and the main batteries are all junked up. We'll need all sorts of repairs, but I guess we're lucky at that. You did a good job, Mr. Williams."

Lucky nodded briefly. "Suppose you tell me what happened."

Reval flushed. "I don't know. I hate to say it, but I don't know."

"How about you?" asked Lucky, addressing the other.

Tor Johnson, his large hands nursing the radio back to life, shook his head.

Reval said, "The last clear thoughts I can remember were while we were still inside the cloud layer. I remember nothing after that till I found myself staring at your flash."

Lucky said, "Do you or Johnson use drugs of any kind?"

Johnson looked up angrily. He rumbled, "No. Nothing."

"Then what made you blank out, and both at the same time, too?"

Reval said, "I wish I knew. Look, Mr. Williams, neither one of us is an amateur. Our records as coaster pilots are first class." He groaned. "Or at least we *were* first-class pilots. We'll probably be grounded after this."

"We'll see," said Lucky.

"Say, look," said Bigman, testily, "what's the use of talking about what's over and gone? Where are we now? That's what I want to know. Where are we going?"

Tor Johnson said, "We're 'way off our course. I can tell you that much. It will be five or six hours before we get out to Aphrodite."

"Fat Jupiter and little satellites!" said Bigman, staring at the blackness outside the port in disgust. "Five or six hours in *this* black mess?"

Aphrodite is the largest city on Venus, with a population of over a quarter of a million.

With the *Venus Marvel* still a mile away, the sea about it was lit into green translucence by Aphrodite's lights. In the eerie luminosity the dark, sleek shapes of the rescue vessels, which had been sent out to meet them after radio contact had been established, could be plainly made out. They slipped along, silent companions.

As for Lucky and Bigman, it was their first sight of one of Venus's underwater domed cities. They almost forgot the unpleasantness they had just passed through, in their amazement at the wonderful object before them.

From a distance it seemed an emerald-green, fairyland bubble, shimmering and quivering because of the water between them. Dimly they could make out buildings and the structural webbing of the beams that held up the city dome against the weight of water overhead.

It grew larger and glowed more brightly as they approached. The green grew lighter as the distance of water between them grew less. Aphrodite became less unreal, less fairylandish, but even more magnificent.

Finally they slid into a huge air lock, capable of holding a small fleet of freighters or a large battle cruiser, and waited while the water was pumped out. And when that was done, the *Venus Marvel* was floated out of the lock and into the city on a lift field.

Lucky and Bigman watched as their luggage was removed, shook hands gravely with Reval and Johnson, and took a skimmer to the Hotel Bellevue-Aphrodite.

Bigman looked out of the curved window as their skimmer, its gyro-wings revolving with stately dignity, moved lightly among the city's beams and over its rooftops.

He said, "So this is Venus. Don't know if it's worth going through so much for it, though. I'll never forget that ocean coming up at us!"

Lucky said, "I'm afraid that was just the beginning."

Bigman looked uneasily at his big friend. "You really think so?"

Lucky shrugged. "It depends. Let's see what Evans has to tell us."

The Green Room of the Hotel Bellevue-Aphrodite was just that. The quality of the lighting and the shimmer of it gave the tables and guests the appearance of being suspended beneath the sea. The ceiling was an inverted bowl, below which there turned slowly a large aquarium globe, supported by cunningly placed lift beams. The water in it was laced with strands of Venusian seaweed and in among it writhed colorful "sea ribbons," one of the most beautiful forms of animal life on the planet.

Bigman had come in first, intent on dinner. He was annoyed at the absence of a punch menu, disturbed by the presence of actual human waiters, and resentful over the fact that he was told that diners in the Green Room ate a meal supplied by the management and only that. He was mollified, slightly, when the appetizer turned out to be tasty and the soup, very good.

Then the music started, the domed ceiling gradually came to glowing life, and the aquarium globe began its gentle spinning.

Bigman's mouth fell open; his dinner was forgotten. "Look at that," he said.

Lucky was looking. The sea ribbons were of different lengths, varying from tiny threads two inches long to broad and sinuous belts that stretched a yard or more from end to end. They were all thin, thin as a sheet of paper. They moved by wriggling their bodies into a series of waves that rippled down their full length.

And each one fluoresced; each one sparkled with colored light. It was a tremendous display. Down the sides of each sea ribbon were little glowing spirals of light: crimson, pink, and orange; a few blues and violets scattered through; and one or two striking whites among the larger specimens. All were overcast with the light-green wash of the external light. As they swam, the lines of color snapped and interlaced. To the dazzled eye they seemed to be leaving rainbow trails that washed and sparkled in the water, fading out only to be renewed in still brighter tints.

Bigman turned his attention reluctantly to his dessert. The waiter had called it "jelly seeds," and at first the little fellow had regarded the dish suspiciously. The jelly seeds were soft orange ovals, which clung together just a bit but came up readily enough in the spoon. For a moment they felt dry and tasteless to the tongue, but then, suddenly, they melted into a thick, sirupy liquid that was sheer delight.

"Space!" said the astonished Bigman. "Have you tried the dessert?"

"What?" asked Lucky absently.

"Taste the dessert, will you? It's like thick pineapple juice, only a million times better. . . . What's the matter?"

Lucky said, "We have company."

"Aw, go on." Bigman made a move to turn in his seat as though to inspect the other diners.

Lucky said quietly, "Take it easy," and that froze Bigman.

Bigman heard the soft steps of someone approaching their table. He tried to twist his eyes. His own blaster was in his room, but he had a force knife in his belt pocket. It looked like a watch fob, but it could slice a man in two, if necessary. He fingered it intensely.

A voice behind Bigman said, "May I join you, folks?"

Bigman turned in his seat, force knife palmed and ready for a quick, upward thrust. But the man looked anything but sinister. He was fat, but his clothes fit well. His face was round and his graying hair was carefully combed over the top of his head, though his baldness showed anyway. His eyes were little, blue, and full of what seemed like friendliness. Of course, he had a large, grizzled mustache of the true Venusian fashion.

Lucky said calmly, "Sit down, by all means." His attention seemed entirely centered on the cup of hot coffee that he held cradled in his right hand.

The fat man sat down. His hands rested upon the table. One wrist was exposed, slightly shaded by the palm of the other. For an instant, an oval spot on it darkened and turned black. Within it little yellow grains of light danced and flickered in the familiar patterns of the Big Dipper and of Orion. Then it disappeared, and there was only an innocent plump wrist and the smiling, round face of the fat man above it.

That identifying mark of the Council of Science could be neither forged nor imitated. The method of its controlled appearance by the exertion of will was just about the most closely guarded secret of the Council.

The fat man said, "My name is Mel Morriss."

Lucky said, "I rather thought you were. You've been described to me."

Bigman sat back and returned his force knife to its place. Mel Morriss was head of the Venusian section of the Council. Bigman had heard of him. In a way he was relieved, and in another way he was just a little disappointed. He had expected a fight—perhaps a quick dash of coffee into the fat man's face, the table overturned, and from then on, anything.

Lucky said, "Venus seems an unusual and beautiful place."

"You have observed our fluorescent aquarium?"

"It is very spectacular," said Lucky.

The Venusian councilman smiled and raised a finger. The waiter brought him a hot cup of coffee. Morriss let it cool for a moment, then said softly, "I believe you are disappointed to see me here. You expected other company, I think."

Lucky said coolly, "I had looked forward to an informal conversation with a friend."

"In fact," said Morriss, "you had sent a message to Councilman Evans to meet you here."

"I see you know that."

"Quite. Evans has been under close observation for quite a while. Communications to him are intercepted."

Their voices were low. Even Bigman had trouble hearing them as they faced one another, sipping coffee and allowing no trace of expression in their words.

Lucky said, "You are wrong to do this."

"You speak as his friend?"

"I do."

"And I suppose that, as your friend, he warned you to stay away from Venus."

"You know about that, too, I see?"

"Quite. And you had a near-fatal accident in landing on Venus. Am I right?"

"You are. You're implying that Evans feared some such event?"

"Feared it? Great space, Starr, your friend Evans *engineered* that accident."

Chapter 3

YEAST!

LUCKY'S EXPRESSION REMAINED IMPASSIVE. Not by so much as an eye flicker did he betray any concern. "Details, please," he said.

Morriss was smiling again, half his mouth hidden by his preposterous Venusian mustache. "Not here, I'm afraid."

"Name your place, then."

"One moment." Morriss looked at his watch. "In just about a minute, the show will begin. There'll be dancing by sealight."

"Sealight?"

"The globe above will shine dim green. People will get up to dance. We will get up with them and quietly leave."

"You sound as though we are in danger at the moment."

Morriss said gravely, *"You* are. I assure you that since you entered Aphrodite, our men have never let you out of their sight."

A genial voice rang out suddenly. It seemed to come from the crystal centerpiece on the table. From the direction in which other diners turned their attention, it obviously came from the crystal centerpiece on every table.

It said, "Ladies and gentlemen, welcome to the Green

Room. Have you eaten well? For your added pleasure, the management is proud to present the magnetonic rhythms of Tobe Tobias and his—"

As the voice spoke, the lights went out and the remainder of its words were drowned in a rising sigh of wonder that came from the assembled guests, most of whom were fresh from Earth. The aquarium globe in the ceiling was suddenly a luminous emerald green and the sea-ribbon glow was sharply brilliant. The globe assumed a faceted appearance so that, as it turned, drifting shadows circled the room in a soft, almost hypnotic fashion. The sound of music, drawn almost entirely from the weird, husky sound boxes of a variety of magnetonic instruments, grew louder. The notes were produced by rods of various shapes being moved in skillful patterns through the magnetic field that surrounded each instrument.

Men and women were rising to dance. There was the rustle of much motion and the sibilance of laughing whispers. A touch on Lucky's sleeve brought first him, and then Bigman, to their feet.

Lucky and Bigman followed Morriss silently. One by one, grim-faced figures fell in behind them. It was almost as though they were materializing out of the draperies. They remained far enough away to look innocent, but each, Lucky felt sure, had his hand near the butt of a blaster. No mistake about it. Mel Morriss of the Venusian section of the Council of Science took the situation very much in earnest.

Lucky looked about Morriss's apartment with approval. It was not lavish, although it was comfortable. Living in it, one could forget that a hundred yards above was a translucent dome beyond which was a hundred yards of shallow, carbonated ocean, followed by a hundred miles of alien, unbreathable atmosphere.

What actually pleased Lucky most was the collection of book films that overflowed one alcove.

He said, "You're a biophysicist, Dr. Morriss?" Automatically, he used the professional title.

Morriss said, "Yes."

"I did biophysical work myself at the academy," said Lucky.

"I know," said Morriss. "I read your paper. It was good work. May I call you David, by the way?"

"It's my first name," conceded the Earthman, "but everyone calls me Lucky."

Bigman, meanwhile, had opened one of the film holders, unreeled a bit of the film, and held it to the light. He shuddered and replaced it.

He said belligerently to Morriss, "You sure don't look like a scientist."

"I imagine not," said Morriss, unoffended. "That helps, you know."

Lucky knew what he meant. In these days, when science really permeated all human society and culture, scientists could no longer restrict themselves to their laboratories. It was for that reason that the Council of Science had been born. Originally it was intended only as an advisory body to help the government on matters of galactic importance, where only trained scientists could have sufficient information to make intelligent decisions. More and more it had become a crime-fighting agency, a counterespionage system. Into its own hands it was drawing more and more of the threads of government. Through its activities there might grow, someday, a great Empire of the Milky Way in which all men might live in peace and harmony.

So it came about that, as members of the Council had to fulfill many duties far removed from pure science, it was better for their success if they didn't look particularly like scientists—as long, that is, as they had the brains of scientists.

Lucky said, "Would you begin, sir, by filling me in on the details of the troubles here?"

"How much were you told on Earth?"

"The barest sketch. I would prefer to trust the man on the scene for the rest."

Morriss smiled with more than a trace of irony. "Trust the man on the scene? That's not the usual

attitude of the men in the central office. They send their
own trouble shooters, and men such as Evans arrive."

"And myself, too," said Lucky.

"Your case is a little different. We all know of your
accomplishments on Mars last year* and the good piece
of work you've just finished in the asteroids."†

Bigman crowed, "You should have been *with* him if
you think you know all about it."

Lucky reddened slightly. He said hastily, "Never
mind now, Bigman. Let's not have any of your yarns."

They were all in large armchairs, Earth-manu-
factured, soft and comfortable. There was something
about the reflected sound of their voices that, to
Lucky's practiced ear, was good evidence that the
apartment was insulated and spy-shielded.

Morriss lit a cigarette and offered one to the others
but was refused. "How much do you know about
Venus, Lucky?"

Lucky smiled. "The usual things one learns in school.
Just to go over a few things quickly, it's the second
closest planet to the sun and is about sixty-seven million miles from it. It's the closest world to Earth and
can come to within twenty-six million miles of the
home planet. It's just a little smaller than Earth, with
a gravity about five sixths Earth-normal. It goes around
the sun in about seven and a half months and its day is
about thirty-six hours long. It's surface temperature
is a little higher than Earth's but not much, because of
the clouds. Also because of the clouds, it has no
seasons to speak of. It is covered by ocean, which is,
in turn, covered with seaweed. Its atmosphere is carbon
dioxide and nitrogen and is unbreathable. How is that,
Dr. Morriss?"

"You pass with high marks," said the biophysicist,
"but I was asking about Venusian society rather than
about the planet itself."

"Well, now, that's more difficult. I know, of course,

*See *David Starr, Space Ranger* (New York, Signet, 1971).
†See *Lucky Starr and the Pirates of the Asteroids* (New York,
Signet, 1971).

that humans live in domed cities in the shallower parts of the ocean, and, as I can see for myself, Venusian city life is quite advanced—far beyond Martian city life, for instance."

Bigman yelled, "Hey!"

Morriss turned his little twinkling eyes on the Martian. "You disagree with your friend?"

Bigman hesitated. "Well, maybe not, but he doesn't have to say so."

Lucky smiled and went on, "Venus is a fairly developed planet. I think there are about fifty cities on it and a total population of six million. Your exports are dried seaweed, which I am told is excellent fertilizer, and dehydrated yeast bricks for animal food."

"Still fairly good," said Morriss. "How was your dinner at the Green Room, gentlemen?"

Lucky paused at the sudden change of topic, then said, "Very good. Why do you ask?"

"You'll see in a moment. What did you have?"

Lucky said, "I couldn't say, exactly. It was the house meal. I should guess we had a kind of beef goulash with a rather interesting sauce and a vegetable I didn't recognize. There was a fruit salad, I believe, before that and a spicy variety of tomato soup."

Bigman broke in. "And jelly seeds for dessert."

Morriss laughed hootingly. "You're all wrong, you know," he said. "You had no beef, no fruit, no tomatoes. Not even coffee. You had only one thing to eat. Only one thing. Yeast!"

"What?" shrieked Bigman.

For a moment Lucky was startled also. His eyes narrowed and he said, "Are you serious?"

"Of course. It's the Green Room's specialty. They never speak of it, or Earthmen would refuse to eat it. Later on, though, you would have been questioned thoroughly as to how you liked this dish or that, how you thought it might have been improved, and so on. The Green Room is Venus's most valuable experimental station."

Bigman screwed up his small face and yelled vehemently, "I'll have the law on them. I'll make a Council case of it. They can't feed me yeast without telling me, like I was a horse or a cow—or a——"

He ended in a flurry of sputtering.

"I am guessing," said Lucky, "that yeast has some connection with the crime wave on Venus."

"Guessing, are you?" said Morriss, dryly. "Then you haven't read our official reports. I'm not surprised. Earth thinks we are exaggerating here. I assure you, however, we are not. And it isn't merely a crime wave. Yeast, Lucky, yeast! That is the nub and core of everything on this planet."

A self-propelled tender had rolled into the living room with a bubbling percolator and three cups of steaming coffee upon it. The tender stopped at Lucky first, then Bigman. Morriss took the third cup, put his lips to it, then wiped his large mustache appreciatively.

"It will add cream and sugar if you wish, gentlemen," he said.

Bigman looked and sniffed. He said to Morriss with sharp suspicion, "Yeast?"

"No. Real coffee this time. I swear it."

For a moment they sipped in silence; then Morriss said, "Venus, Lucky, is an expensive world to keep up. Our cities must make oxygen out of water, and that takes huge electrolytic stations. Each city requires tremendous power beams to help support the domes against billions of tons of water. The city of Aphrodite uses as much energy in a year as the entire continent of South America, yet it has only a thousandth the population.

"We've got to earn that energy, naturally. We've got to export to Earth in order to obtain power plants, specialized machinery, atomic fuel, and so on. Venus's only product is seaweed, inexhaustible quantities of it. Some we export as fertilizer, but that is scarcely the answer to the problem. Most of our seaweed, however, we use as culture media for yeast, ten thousand and one varieties of yeast."

Bigman's lip curled. "Changing seaweed to yeast isn't much of an improvement."

"Did you find your last meal satisfactory?" asked Morriss.

"Please go on, Dr. Morriss," said Lucky.

Morriss said, "Of course, Mr. Jones is quite cor——"

"Call me Bigman!"

Morriss looked soberly at the small Martian and said, "If you wish. Bigman is quite correct in his low opinion of yeast in general. Our most important strains are suitable only for animal food. But even so, it's highly useful. Yeast-fed pork is cheaper and better than any other kind. The yeast is high in calories, proteins, minerals, and vitamins.

"We have other strains of higher quality, which are used in cases where food must be stored over long periods and with little available space. On long space journeys, for instance, so-called Y-rations are frequently taken.

"Finally, we have our top-quality strains, extremely expensive and fragile growths that go into the menus of the Green Room and with which we can imitate or improve upon ordinary food. None of these are in quantity production, but they will be someday. I imagine you see the whole point of all this, Lucky."

"I think I do."

"I don't," said Bigman belligerently.

Morriss was quick to explain. "Venus will have a monopoly on these luxury strains. No other world will possess them. Without Venus's experience in zymoculture——"

"In what?" asked Bigman.

"In yeast culture. Without Venus's experience in that, no other world could develop such yeasts or maintain them once they did obtain them. So you see that Venus could build a tremendously profitable trade in yeast strains as luxury items with all the galaxy. That would be important not only to Venus, but to Earth as well—to the entire Solar Confederation. We are the most overpopulated system in the Galaxy, being the oldest. If we could exchange a pound of yeast for a ton of grain, things would be well for us."

Lucky had been listening patiently to Morriss's lecture. He said, "For the same reason, it would be to the interest of a foreign power, which was anxious to weaken Earth, to ruin Venus's monopoly of yeast."

"You see that, do you? I wish I could persuade the rest of the Council of this living and ever-present danger. If growing strains of yeast were stolen along with some of the knowledge of our developments in yeast culture, the results could be disastrous."

"Very well," said Lucky, "then we come to the important point: Have such thefts occurred?"

"Not yet," said Morriss grimly. "But for six months now we have had a rash of petty pilfering, odd accidents, and queer incidents. Some are merely annoying, or even funny, like the case of the old man who threw half-credit pieces to children and then went frantically to the police, insisting he had been robbed. When witnesses came forward to show that he had given the money away, he nearly went mad with fury, insisting that he had done no such thing. There are more serious accidents, too, like that in which a freight-roller operator released a half-ton bale of weed at the wrong time and killed two men. He insisted later that he had blacked out."

Bigman squealed excitedly, "Lucky! The pilots on the coaster claimed *they* blacked out."

Morriss nodded, "Yes, and I'm almost glad it happened as long as the two of you survived. The Council on Earth may be a bit readier to believe there is something behind all this."

"I suppose," said Lucky, "you suspect hypnotism."

Morriss drew his lips into a grim, humorless smile. "Hypnotism is a mild word, Lucky. Do you know of any hypnotist who can exert his influence at a distance over unwilling subjects? I tell you that some person or persons on Venus possesses the power of complete mental domination over others. They are exerting this power, practicing it, growing more adept in its use. With every day it will grow more difficult to fight them. Perhaps it is already too late!"

Chapter 4

COUNCILMAN ACCUSED!

BIGMAN'S EYES SPARKLED. "It's never too late once Lucky gets going. Where do we start, Lucky?"

Lucky said quietly, "With Lou Evans. I've been waiting for you to mention him, Dr. Morriss."

Morriss's eyebrows drew together; his plump face contracted into a frown. "You're his friend. You want to defend him, I know. It's not a pleasant story. It wouldn't be if it involved any councilman at all—but a friend at that."

Lucky said, "I am not acting out of sentiment only, Dr. Morriss. I knew Lou Evans as well as one man can know another. I know he is incapable of doing anything to harm the Council or Earth."

"Then listen, and judge for yourself. For most of Evans's tour of duty here on Venus, he accomplished nothing. A 'trouble shooter' they called him, which is a pretty word but means nothing."

"No offense, Dr. Morriss, but did you resent his arrival?"

"No, of course not. I just saw no point in it. We here have grown old on Venus. We have the experience. What do they expect a youngster, new from Earth, to accomplish?"

"A fresh approach is helpful sometimes."

"Nonsense. I tell you, Lucky, the trouble is that

Earth headquarters don't consider our problem important. Their purpose in sending Evans was to have him
give it a quick glance, whitewash it, and return to tell
them it was nothing."

"I know the Council on Earth better than that. You
do, too."

But the grumbling Venusian went on. "Anyway,
three weeks ago, this man Evans asked to see some of
the classified data concerning yeast-strain growth. The
men in the industry objected."

"Objected?" said Lucky. "It was a councilman's request."

"True, but yeast-strain men are secretive. You don't
make requests like that. Even councilmen don't. They
asked Evans why he wanted the information. He refused
to tell them. They forwarded his request to me, and I
quashed it."

"On what grounds?" demanded Lucky.

"He wouldn't tell me his reasons either, and while
I'm senior councilman on Venus, nobody in my organization will have secrets from me. But your friend Lou
Evans then did something I had not expected. He
stole the data. He used his position as councilman to
get inside a restricted area in the yeast-research plants,
and he left with microfilms inside his boot."

"Surely he had a good reason."

"He did," said Morriss, "he did. The microfilms
dealt with the nutrient formulas required for the
nourishment of a new and very tricky strain of yeast.
Two days later a workman making up one component
of that mixture introduced a trace of mercury salt. The
yeast died, and six months' work was ruined. The workman swore he'd done no such thing, but he had. Our
psychiatrists psychoprobed him. By now, you see, we
had a pretty good notion of what to expect. He'd had
a blackout period. The enemy still hasn't stolen the
strain of yeast, but they're getting closer. Right?"

Lucky's brown eyes were hard. "I can see the obvious
theory. Lou Evans had deserted to the enemy, whoever
he is."

"Sirians," blurted Morriss. "I'm sure of it."

"Maybe," admitted Lucky. The inhabitants of the planets of Sirius had, for centuries now, been Earth's most fervent enemies. It was easy to blame them. "Maybe. Lou Evans deserted to them, let us say, and agreed to get data for them that would enable them to start trouble inside the yeast factories. Little troubles at first, which would pave the way for larger troubles."

"Yes, that's my theory. Can you propose any other?

"Couldn't Councilman Evans himself be under mental domination?"

"Not likely, Lucky. We have many cases in our files now. No one who has suffered from mental domination has blacked out for longer than half an hour, and all gave clear indication under the psychoprobe of periods of total amnesia. Evans would have had to be under mental domination for two days to have done what he did, and he gave no signs of amnesia."

"He was examined?"

"He certainly was. When a man is found with classified material in his possession—caught in the act, as it were—steps have to be taken. I wouldn't care if he were a hundred times a councilman. He was examined, and I, personally, put him on probation. When he broke it to send some message on his own equipment, we tapped his scrambler and made sure he'd do it no more—or, at least, not without our intercepting whatever he sent or received. The message he sent you was his last. We're through playing with him. He's under confinement now. I'm preparing my report for central headquarters, a thing I should have done before this, and I'm requesting his removal from office and trial for corruption, or, perhaps, for treason."

"Before you do that——" said Lucky.

"Yes?"

"Let me speak to him."

Morriss rose, smiling ironically. "You wish to? Certainly. I'll take you to him. He's in this building. In fact, I'd like to have you hear his defense."

They passed up a ramp, quiet guards snapping to attention and saluting.

Bigman stared at them curiously. "Is this a prison or what?"

"It's a kind of prison on these levels," said Morriss. "We make buildings serve many purposes on Venus."

They stepped into a small room, and suddenly, quite without warning, Bigman burst into loud laughter.

Lucky, unable to repress a smile, said, "What's the matter, Bigman?"

"No—nothing much," panted the little fellow, his eyes moist. "It's just that you look so funny, Lucky, standing there with your bare upper lip hanging out. After all those mustaches I've been watching, you look deformed. You look as though someone had taken a whiffgun and blown off the mustache you should have had."

Morriss smiled at that and brushed his own grizzled mustache with the back of his hand, self-consciously and a little proudly.

Lucky's smile expanded. "Funny," he said, "I was thinking exactly the same about you, Bigman."

Morriss said, "We'll wait here. They're bringing Evans now." His finger moved away from a small push-button signal.

Lucky looked about the room. It was smaller than Morriss's own room, more impersonal. Its only furniture consisted of several upholstered chairs plus a sofa, a low table in the center of the room, and two higher tables near the false windows. Behind each of the false windows was a cleverly done seascape. On one of the two high tables was an aquarium; on the other, two dishes, one containing small dried peas and the other, a black, greasy substance.

Bigman's eyes automatically started following Lucky's about the room.

He said, suddenly, "Say, Lucky, what's this?

He half-ran to the aquarium, bending low, peering into its depths. "Look at it, will you?"

"It's just one of the pet V-frogs the men keep about

here," said Morriss. "It's a rather good specimen. Haven't you ever seen one?"

"No," said Lucky. He joined Bigman at the aquarium, which was two feet square and about three feet deep. The water in it was criss-crossed with feathery fronds of weed.

Bigman said, "It doesn't bite or anything, does it?" He was stirring the water with a forefinger and bending close to peer inside.

Lucky's head came down next to Bigman's. The V-frog stared back at them solemnly. It was a little creature, perhaps eight inches long, with a triangular head into which two bulging black eyes were set. It rested on six little padded feet drawn up close to its body. Each foot had three long toes in front and one behind. Its skin was green and froglike, and there were frilly fins, which vibrated rapidly, running down the center line of its back. In place of a mouth it had a beak, strong, curved and parrotlike.

As Lucky and Bigman watched, the V-frog started rising in the water. Its feet remained on the floor of the aquarium, but its legs stretched out like extendible stilts, as its numerous leg joints straightened. It stopped rising just as its head was about to pierce the surface.

Morriss, who had joined them and was staring fondly at the little beast, said, "It doesn't like to get out of the water. Too much oxygen in the air. They enjoy oxygen, but only in moderation. They're mild, pleasant little things."

Bigman was delighted. There was virtually no native animal life on Mars, and living creatures of this sort were a real novelty to him.

"Where do they live?" he asked.

Morriss put a finger down into the water and stroked the V-frog's head. The V-frog permitted it, closing its dark eyes in spasmodic motions that might have meant delight, for all they could guess.

Morriss said, "They congregate in the seaweed in fairly large numbers. They move around in it as though it were a forest. Their long toes can hold individual stems, and their beaks can tear the toughest fronds. They could probably make a mean dent in a man's finger, but I've never known one of them to bite. I'm amazed you haven't seen one yet. The hotel has a whole collection of them, real family groups, on display. You haven't seen it?"

"We've scarcely had the chance," said Lucky dryly.

Bigman stepped quickly to the other table, picked up a pea, dipped it into the black grease, and brought it back. He held it out temptingly, and with infinite care the V-frog's beak thrust out of the water and took the morsel from Bigman's fingers. Bigman crowed his delight:

"Did you see that?" he demanded.

Morriss smiled fondly, as though at the tricks of a child. "The little imp. They'll eat that all day. Look at him gobble it."

The V-frog was crunching away. A small black droplet leaked out of one side of its beak, and at once the little creature's legs folded up again as it moved down through the water. The beak opened and the little black droplet was caught.

"What is the stuff?" asked Lucky.

"Peas dipped in axle grease," said Morriss. "Grease is a great delicacy for them, like sugar for us. They hardly ever find pure hydrocarbon in their natural habitat. They love it so, I wouldn't be surprised if they let themselves be captured just to get it."

"How are they captured, by the way?"

"Why, when the seaweed trawlers gather up their seaweed, there are always V-frogs collected with it. Other animals, too."

Bigman was saying eagerly, "Hey, Lucky, let's you and I get one——"

He was interrupted by a pair of guards, who entered stiffly. Between them stood a lanky, blond young man.

Lucky sprang to his feet. "Lou! Lou, old man!" He held out his hand, smiling.

For a moment it seemed as though the other might

respond. A flicker of joy rose to the newcomer's eyes.

It faded quickly. His arms remained stiffly and coldly at his side. He said flatly, "Hello, Starr."

Lucky's hand dropped reluctantly. He said, "I haven't seen you since we graduated." He paused. What could one say next to an old friend?

The blond councilman seemed aware of the incongruity of the situation. Nodding curtly to the flanking guards, he said with macabre humor, "There've been some changes made since then." Then, with a spasmodic tightening of his thin lips, he went on, "Why did you come? Why didn't you stay away? I asked you to."

"I can't stay away when a friend's in trouble, Lou."

"Wait till your help is asked for."

Morriss said, "I think you're wasting your time, Lucky. You're thinking of him as a councilman. I suggest that he's a renegade."

The plump Venusian said the word through clenched teeth, bringing it down like a lash. Evans reddened slowly but said nothing.

Lucky said, "I'll need proof to the last atom before I admit any such word in connection with Councilman Evans." His voice came down hard on the word "councilman."

Lucky sat down. For a long moment he regarded his friend soberly, and Evans looked away.

Lucky said, "Dr. Morriss, ask the guards to leave. I will be responsible for Evans's security."

Morriss lifted an eyebrow at Lucky, then after an instant's thought, gestured to the guards.

Lucky said, "If you don't mind, Bigman, just step into the next room, will you?"

Bigman nodded and left.

Lucky said gently, "Lou, there are only three of us here now. You, I, Dr. Morriss; that's all. Three men of the Council of Science. Suppose we start fresh. Did you remove classified data concerning yeast manufacture from their place in the files?"

Lou Evans said, "I did."

"Then you must have had a reason. What was it?"

"Now look. I stole the papers. I say *stole*. I admit that much. What more do you want? I had no reason for doing it. I just did it. Now drop it. Get away from me. Leave me alone." His lips were trembling.

Morriss said, "You wanted to hear his defense, Lucky. That's it. He has none."

Lucky said, "I suppose you know that there was an accident inside the yeast plants, shortly after you took those papers, involving just the strain of yeast the papers dealt with."

"I know all that," said Evans.

"How do you explain it?"

"I have no explanation."

Lucky was watching Evans closely, searching for some sign of the good-natured, fun-loving, steel-nerved youth he remembered so well at the academy. Except for a new mustache, grown according to Venusian fashion, the man Lucky saw now resembled the memory as far as mere physical appearance was concerned. The same long-boned limbs, the blond hair cut short, the angular, pointed chin, the flat-bellied, athletic body. But otherwise? Evans's eyes moved restlessly from spot to spot; his lips quivered dryly; his fingernails were bitten and ragged.

Lucky struggled with himself before he could put the next blunt question. It was a friend he was talking to, a man he had known well, a man whose loyalty he never had questioned, and on whose loyalty he would have staked his own life without thought.

He said, "Lou, have you sold out?"

Evans said in a dull, toneless voice, "No comment."

"Lou, I'm asking you again. First, I want you to know that I'm on your side no matter what you've done. If you've failed the Council, there must be a reason. Tell us that reason. If you've been drugged or forced, either physically or mentally, if you've been blackmailed or if someone close to you has been threatened, tell us. For Earth's sake, Lou, even if you've been tempted with offers of money or power, even if it's as crude as that, tell us. There's no error you can have made that can't be at least partially retrieved by frankness now. What about it?"

For a moment, Lou Evans seemed moved. His blue eyes lifted in pain to his friend's face. "Lucky," he began, "I——"

Then the softness in him seemed to die, and he cried, "No comment, Starr, no comment."

Morriss, arms folded, said, "That's it, Lucky. That's his attitude. Only he has information and we want it, and, by Venus, we'll get it one way or another."

Lucky said, "Wait——"

Morriss said, "We can't wait. Get that through your head. There is no time. No time at all. These so-called accidents have been getting more serious as they get closer to their objective. We need to break this thing *now.*" And his pudgy fist slammed down on the arm of his chair, just as the communo shrilled its signal.

Morriss frowned. "Emergency signal! What in space——"

He flicked the circuit open, put the receiver to his ear.

"Morriss speaking. What is it? . . . *What?* . . . *WHAT?*"

He let the receiver fall, and his face, as it turned toward Lucky, was a doughy, unhealthy white.

"There's a hypnotized man at lock number twenty-three," he choked out.

Lucky's lithe body tightened like a steel spring. "What do you mean by 'lock'? Are you referring to the dome?"

Morriss nodded and managed to say, "I said the accidents are getting more serious. This time, the sea dome. That man may—at any moment—let the ocean into—Aphrodite!"

Chapter 5

"BEWARE WATER!"

FROM THE SPEEDING GYROCAR, Lucky caught glimpses of the mighty dome overhead. A city built under water, he reflected, requires engineering miracles to be practical.

There were domed cities in many places in the solar system. The oldest and most famous were on Mars. But on Mars, gravity was only two fifths of Earth normal, and pressing down on the Martian domes was only a rarefied, wispy atmosphere.

Here on Venus, gravity was five sixths Earth normal, and the Venusian domes were topped with water. Even though the domes were built in shallow sea so that their tops nearly broke surface at low tide, it was still a matter of supporting millions of tons of water.

Lucky, like most Earthmen (and Venusians, too, for that matter), tended to take such achievements of mankind for granted. But now, with Lou Evans returned to confinement and the problem involving him momentarily dismissed, Lucky's agile mind was putting thoughts together and craving knowledge on this new matter.

He said, "How is the dome supported, Dr. Morriss?"

The fat Venusian had recovered some of his composure. The gyrocar he was driving hurtled toward the threatened sector. His words were still tight and grim.

He said, "Diamagnetic force fields in steel housings. It looks as though steel beams are supporting the dome, but that's not so. Steel just isn't strong enough. It's the force fields that do it."

Lucky looked down at the city streets below, filled with people and life. He said, "Have there ever been any accidents of this type before?"

Morriss groaned, "Great space, not like this. . . . We'll be there in five minutes."

"Are any precautions taken against accidents?" Lucky went on stolidly.

"Of course there are. We have a system of alarms and automatic field adjusters that are as foolproof as we can manage. And the whole city is built in segments. Any local failure in the dome brings down sections of transite, backed by subsidiary fields."

"Then the city won't be destroyed, even if the ocean is let in. Is that right? And this is well known to the populations?"

"Certainly. The people know they're protected, but still, man, a good part of the city will be ruined. There's bound to be some loss of life, and property damage will be terrific. Worse still, if men can be controlled into doing this once, they can be controlled into doing it again."

Bigman, the third man in the gyrocar, stared anxiously at Lucky. The tall Earthman was abstracted, and his brows were knit into a hard frown.

Then Morriss grunted, "Here we are!" The car decelerated rapidly to a jarring halt.

Bigman's watch said two-fifteen, but that meant nothing. Venus's night was eighteen hours long, and here under the dome there was neither day nor night.

Artificial lights blossomed now as they always did. Buildings loomed clearly as always. If the city seemed different in any way, it was in the actions of its inhabitants. They were swirling out of the various sections of the city. News of the crisis had spread by the mysterious magic of word of mouth, and they were flocking to see the sight, morbidly curious, as though going to a show or a circus parade, or as men on Earth would flock for seats at a magnetonic concert.

Police held back the rumbling crowds and beat out a path for Morriss and the two with him. Already a thick partition of cloudy transite had moved down, blocking off the section of the city that was threatened by deluge.

Morriss shepherded Lucky and Bigman through a large door. The noise of the crowd muffled and faded behind them. Inside the building a man stepped hastily toward Morriss.

"Dr. Morriss——" he began.

Morriss looked up and snapped out hasty introductions. "Lyman Turner, chief engineer. David Starr of the Council. Bigman Jones."

Then, at some signal from another part of the room, he dashed off, his heavy body making surprising speed. He called out over his shoulder as he started, "Turner will take care of you two."

Turner yelled, "Just a minute, Dr. Morriss!" but the yell went unheard.

Lucky gestured to Bigman, and the little Martian raced after the Venusian councilman.

"Is he going to bring Dr. Morriss back?" asked Turner worriedly, stroking a rectangular box he carried suspended from a strap over one shoulder. He had a gaunt face and red-brown hair, a prominently hooked nose, a scattering of freckles, and a wide mouth. There was trouble in his face.

"No," said Lucky. "Morriss may be needed out there. I just gave my friend the high sign to stick closely to him."

"I don't know what good that will do," muttered the engineer. "I don't know what good anything will do." He put a cigarette to his mouth and absently held one out to Lucky. Lucky's refusal went unnoticed for a few moments, and Turner stood there, holding the plastic container of smokes at arm's length, lost in a thoughtful world of his own.

Lucky said, "They're evacuating the threatened sector, I suppose?"

Turner took back his cigarettes with a start, then puffed strongly at the one between his lips. He dropped it and pressed it out with the sole of his shoe.

"They are," he said, "but I don't know . . ." and his voice faded out.

Lucky said, "The partition is safely across the city, isn't it?"

"Yes, yes," muttered the engineer.

Lucky waited a moment, then said, "But you're not satisfied. What is it you were trying to tell Dr. Morriss?"

The engineer looked hastily at Lucky, hitched at the black box he carried and said, "Nothing. Forget it."

They were off by themselves in a corner of the room. Men were entering now, dressed in pressure suits with the helmets removed, mopping perspiring foreheads. Parts of sentences drifted to their ears:

". . . not more than three thousand people left. We're using all the interlocks now . . ."

". . . can't get to him. Tried everything. His wife is on the etherics now, pleading with him . . ."

"Darn it, he's got the lever in his hand. All he has to do is pull it and we're . . ."

"If we could only get close enough to blast him down! If we were only sure he wouldn't see us first and . . ."

Turner seemed to listen to all of it with a grisly fascination, but he remained in the corner. He lit another cigarette and ground it out.

He burst out savagely, "Look at that crowd out there. It's fun to them. Excitement! I don't know what to do. I tell you, I don't." He hitched the black box he carried into a more comfortable position and held it close.

"What is that?" asked Lucky peremptorily.

Turner looked down, stared at the box as though he were seeing it for the first time, then said, "It's my computer. A special portable model I designed myself." For a moment pride drowned the worry in his voice. "There's not another one in the galaxy like it. I always carry it around. That's how I know——" And he stopped again.

Lucky said in a hard voice. "All right, Turner, what do you know? I want you to start talking. Now!"

The young councilman's hand came lightly to rest upon the engineer's shoulder, and then his grip began to tighten just a bit.

Turner looked up, startled, and the other's calm, brown eyes held him. "What's your name again?" he said.

"I'm David Starr."

Turner's eyes brightened. "The man they call 'Lucky' Starr?"

"That's right."

"All right, then, I'll tell you, but I can't talk loudly. It's dangerous."

He began whispering, and Lucky's head bent toward him. Both were completely disregarded by the busily hurrying men who entered and left the room.

Turner's low words flooded out now as though he were glad to be able to get rid of them. He said, "The walls of the city dome are double, see. Each wall is made of transite, which is the toughest, strongest silicone plastic known to science. And it's backed by force beams. It can stand immense pressures. It's completely insoluble. It doesn't etch. No form of life will grow on it. It won't change chemically as a result of anything in the Venusian ocean. In between the two parts of the double wall is compressed carbon dioxide. That serves to break the shock wave if the outer wall should give way, and of course the inner wall is strong enough to hold the water by itself. Finally, there's a honeycomb of partitions between the walls so that only small portions of the in-between will be flooded in case of any break."

"It's an elaborate system," said Lucky.

"Too elaborate," said Turner bitterly. "An earthquake, or a Venusquake, rather, might split the dome in two, but nothing else can touch it. And there are no Venusquakes in this part of the planet." He stopped to light still another cigarette. His hands were trembling. "What's more, every square foot of the dome is wired to instruments that continually measure the humidity between the walls. The slightest crack anywhere and the needles of those instruments jump. Even if the crack is microscopic and completely invisible, they jump. Then bells ring and sirens sound. Everyone yells, 'Beware water!' "

He grinned crookedly. "Beware water! That's a laugh. I've been on the job ten years, and in all that time the instruments registered only five times. In every case repairs took less than an hour. You pin a diving bell on the affected part of the dome, pump out the water, fuse the transite, add another gob of the stuff, let it cool. After that, the dome is stronger than before. Beware water! We've never had even a drop leak through."

Lucky said, "I get the picture. Now get to the point."

"The point is overconfidence, Mr. Starr. We've partitioned off the dangerous sector, but how strong is the partition? We always counted on the outer wall's going gradually, springing a small leak. The water would trickle in, and we always knew that we would have plenty of time to get ready for it. No one ever thought that someday a lock might be opened wide. The water will come in like a fat steel bar moving a mile a second. It will hit the sectional transite barrier like a spaceship at full acceleration."

"You mean it won't hold?"

"I mean no one has ever worked out the problem. No one has ever computed the forces involved—until half an hour ago. Then I did, just to occupy my time while all this is going on. I had my computer. I always have it with me. So I made a few assumptions and went to work."

"And it won't hold?"

"I'm not certain. I don't know how good some of my assumptions are, but I think it won't hold. I think it won't. So what do we do? If the barrier doesn't hold, Aphrodite is done. The whole city. You and I and a quarter of a million people. Everybody. Those crowds outside that are so excited and thrilled are doomed once that man's hand pulls downward on the switch it holds."

Lucky was staring at the man with horror. "How long have you known this?"

The engineer blurted in immediate self-defense, "Half an hour. *But what can I do?* We can't put subsea suits on a quarter of a million people! I was thinking of talking to Morriss and maybe getting some of the important people in town protected, or some of the women and children. I wouldn't know how to pick which ones to save, but maybe something should be done. What do you think?"

"I'm not sure."

The engineer went on, harrowed. "I thought maybe I could put on a suit and get out of here. Get out of the city altogether. There won't be proper guards at the exits at a time like this."

Lucky backed away from the quivering engineer, his eyes narrowed. "Great Galaxy! I've been blind!"

And he turned and dashed out of the room, his mind tingled with a desperate thought.

Chapter 6

TOO LATE!

BIGMAN FELT DIZZILY HELPLESS in the confusion. Hanging as closely as he could to the coattails of the restless Morriss, he found himself trotting from group to group, listening to breathless conversations which he did not always understand because of his ignorance about Venus.

Morriss had no opportunity to rest. Each new minute brought a new man, a new report, a new decision. It was only twenty minutes since Bigman had run off after Morriss, and already a dozen plans had been proposed and discarded.

One man, just returned from the threatened sector, was saying with pounding breath, "They've got the spy rays trained on him, and we can make him out. He's just sitting with the lever in his hand. We beamed his wife's voice in at him through the etherics, then through the public-address system, then through loud-speaker from outside. I don't think he hears her. At least he doesn't move."

Bigman bit his lip. What would Lucky do if he were here? The first thought that had occurred to Bigman was to get behind the man—Poppnoe, his name was—and shoot him down. But that was the first thought everyone had had, and it had been instantly discarded. The man at the lever had closed himself off, and the dome-control chambers were carefully designed to prevent any form of tampering. Each entrance was thoroughly wired, the alarms being internally powered. That precaution was now working in reverse—to Aphrodite's peril rather than its protection.

At the first clang, at the first signal gleam, Bigman was sure, the lever would be driven home and Venus's ocean would charge inward upon Aphrodite. It could not be risked while evacuation was incomplete.

Someone had suggested poison gas, but Morriss had shaken his head without explanations. Bigman thought he knew what the Venusian must be thinking. The man at the lever was not sick or mad or malevolent, but under mental control. That fact meant that there were two enemies. The man at the lever, considered by himself, might weaken from the gas past the point where he would be physically capable of pulling the lever, but before that the weakening would be reflected in his mind, and the men in control would work their tool's arm muscles quickly enough.

"What are they waiting for, anyway?" growled Morriss under his breath, while the perspiration rolled down his cheeks in streams. "If I could only train an atom cannon at the spot."

Bigman knew why that was impossible, too. An atom cannon trained to hit the man from the closest approach possible would require enough power to go through a quarter mile of architecture and would damage the dome enough to bring on the very danger they were trying to avoid.

He thought, Where *is* Lucky, anyway? Aloud he said, "If you can't get this fellow, what about the controls?"

"What do you mean?" said Morris.

"I mean, gimmick the lever. It takes power to open the lock, doesn't it? What if the power is cut?"

"Nice thought, Bigman. But each lock has its own emergency power generator on the spot."

"Can't it be closed off from anywhere?"

"How? He's closed off in there, with every cubic foot set off with alarms."

Bigman looked up and, in vision, seemed to see the mighty ocean that covered them. He said, "This is a closed-in city, like on Mars. We've got to pump air all over. Don't you do that, too?"

Morriss brought a handkerchief to his forehead and wiped it slowly. He stared at the little Martian. "The ventilating ducts?"

"Yes. There's got to be one to that place with the lock, doesn't there?"

"Of course."

"And isn't there someplace along the line where a wire can be wrenched loose or cut or *something?*"

"Wait a while. A microbomb shoved along the duct, instead of the poison gas we were talking about———"

"That's not sure enough," said Bigman impatiently. "Send a man. You need big ducts for an underwater city, don't you? Won't they hold a man?"

"They're not as big as all that," said Morriss.

Bigman swallowed painfully. It cost him a great deal to make the next statement. "I'm not as big as all that, either. Maybe I'll fit."

And Morriss, staring down wide-eyed at the pint-size Martian, said, "Venus! You might. You might! Come with me!"

From the appearance of the streets of Aphrodite, it seemed as though not a man or woman or child in the city was sleeping. Just outside the transite partition and surrounding the "rescue headquarters" building, people choked every avenue and turned them into black masses of chattering humanity. Chains had been set up, and behind them policemen with stunguns paced restlessly.

Lucky, having emerged from rescue headquarters at what amounted to a dead run, was brought up sharply by those chains. A hundred impressions burst in on him. There was the brilliant sign in lucite curlicues, set high in Aphrodite's sky with no visible support. It turned slowly and said: APHRODITE, BEAUTY SPOT OF VENUS, WELCOMES YOU.

Close by, a line of men were moving on in file. They

were carrying odd objects—stuffed brief cases, jewel boxes, clothes slung over their arms. One by one, they were climbing into skimmers. It was obvious who and what they were: escapees from within the threatened zone, passing through the lock with whatever they could carry that seemed most important to them. The evacuation was obviously well under way. There were no women and children in the line.

Lucky shouted to a passing policeman, "Is there a skimmer I can use?"

The policeman looked up. "No, sir, all being used."

Lucky said impatiently, "Council business."

"Can't help it. Every skimmer in town is being used for those guys." His thumb jerked toward the moving file of men in the middle distance.

"It's important. I've got to get out of here."

"Then you'll have to walk," said the policeman.

Lucky gritted his teeth with vexation. There was no way of getting through the crowd on foot or on wheels. It had to be by air and it had to be *now*.

"Isn't there anything available I can use? Anything?" He was scarcely speaking to the policeman, more to his own impatient self, angry at having been so simply duped by the enemy.

But the policeman answered wryly, "Unless you want to use a hopper."

"A hopper? Where?" Lucky's eyes blazed.

"I was just joking," said the policeman.

"But *I'm* not. Where's the hopper?"

There were several in the basement of the building they had left. They were disassembled. Four men were impressed to help and the best-looking machine was assembled in the open. The nearest of the crowd watched curiously, and a few shouted jocularly, "Jump it, hopper!"

It was the old cry of the hopper races. Five years ago it had been a fad that had swept the solar system: races over broken, barrier-strewn courses. While the craze lasted, Venus was most enthusiastic. Probably half the houses in Aphrodite had had hoppers in the basement.

Lucky checked the micropile. It was active. He started the motor and set the gyroscope spinning. The hopper straightened immediately and stood stiffly upright on its single leg.

Hoppers are probably the most grotesque forms of transportation ever invented. They consist of a curved body, just large enough to hold a man at the controls. There was a four-bladed rotor above and a single metal leg, rubber-tipped, below. It looked like some giant wading bird gone to sleep with one leg folded under its body.

Lucky touched the leap knob and the hopper's leg retracted. Its body sank till it was scarcely seven feet from the ground while the leg moved up into the hollow tube that pierced the hopper just behind the control panel. The leg was released at the moment of maximum retraction with a loud click, and the hopper sprang thirty feet into the air.

The rotating blades above the hopper kept it hovering for long seconds at the top of its jump. For those seconds, Lucky could get a view of the people now immediately below him. The crowd extended outward for half a mile, and that meant several hops. Lucky's lips tightened. Precious minutes would vanish.

The hopper was coming down now, its long leg extended. The crowd beneath the descending hopper tried to scatter, but they didn't have to. Four jets of compressed air blew men aside just sufficiently, and the leg hurtled down harmlessly to the ground.

The foot hit concrete and retracted. For a flash Lucky could see the startled faces of the people about him, and then the hopper was moving up again.

Lucky had to admit the excitement of hopper racing. As a youngster, he'd participated in several. The expert "hop rider" could twist his curious mount in unbelievable patterns, finding leg room where none seemed to exist. Here, in the domed cities of Venus, the races must have been tame compared to the bone-breakers in the vast, open arenas of rocky, broken ground on Earth.

In four hops Lucky had cleared the crowd. He cut

the motors, and in a series of small, dribbling jumps the hopper came to a halt. Lucky leaped out. Air travel might still be impossible, but now he could commandeer some form of groundcar.

But more time would be lost.

Bigman panted and paused for a moment to get his breath. Things had happened quickly; he had been rushed along in a tide that was still whirling him onward.

Twenty minutes before, he had made his suggestion to Morriss. Now he was enclosed in a tube that tightened about his body and drenched him with darkness.

He inched along on his elbows again, working his way deeper. Momentarily he would stop to use the small flash whose pinpoint illumination showed him milky walls ahead, narrowing to nothing. In one sleeve, against his wrist, he held a hastily scrawled diagram.

Morriss had shaken his hand before Bigman had half-clambered, half-jumped, into the opening at one side of a pumping station. The rotors of the huge fan had been stilled, the air currents stopped.

Morriss had muttered, "I hope *that* doesn't set him off," and then he had shaken hands.

Bigman had grinned back after a fashion, and then he crawled his way into the darkness while the others left. No one felt it necessary to mention the obvious. Bigman was going to be on the wrong side of the transite barrier, the side from which the others were now retreating. If, at any time, the lever at the dome lock plunged down, the incoming water would crush the duct and the walls through which it ran as though they were all so much cardboard.

Bigman wondered, as he squirmed onward, whether he would hear a roar first, whether the surging water would make any hint of its presence known before striking him. He hoped not. He wanted not even a second of waiting. If the water came in, he wanted its work done quickly.

He felt the wall begin to curve. He stopped to consult

his map, his small flash lighting the space about him with a cool gleam. It was the second curve shown in the map they had drawn for him, and now the duct would curve upward.

Bigman worked himself over to his side and bent around the curve to the damage of his temper and the bruising of his flesh.

"Sands of Mars!" he muttered. His thigh muscles ached as he forced his knees against either side of the duct to keep himself from slipping downward again. Inch by inch he clawed his way up the gentle slope.

Morriss had copied the map off the hieroglyphic charts held up before a visiphone transmitter in the Public Works Department of Aphrodite. He had followed the curving colored lines, asked for an interpretation of the markings and symbols.

Bigman reached one of the reinforcing struts that stretched diagonally across the duct. He almost welcomed it as something he could seize, close his hands about, use to take some of the pressure off his aching elbows and knees. He pressed his map back up his sleeve and held the strut with his left hand. His right hand turned his small flash end for end and placed the butt against one end of the strut.

The energy of the enclosed micropile, which ordinarily fed electricity through the small bulb of the flash and turned it into cold light, could also, at another setting of the control, set up a short-range force field through its opposite end. That force field would slice instantaneously through anything composed of mere matter that stood in its way. Bigman set that control and knew that one end of the strut now hung loose.

He switched hands. He worked his slicer to the other end of the strut. Another touch, and it was gone. The strut was loose in his fingers. Bigman worked it past his body, down to his feet, and let it go. It slid and clattered down the duct.

The water still held off. Bigman, panting and squirming, was distantly aware of that. He passed two more struts, another curve. Then the slope leveled off, and finally he reached a set of baffles plainly marked on the map. In all, the ground he had covered was probably less than two hundred yards, but how much time had it taken him?

And still the water held off.

The baffles, blades jutting alternately from either side of the duct to keep the air stream turbulent, were the last landmark. He sliced off each blade with a rapid sweep of his flash butt, and now he had to measure nine feet from the farthest blade. Again he used his flash. It was six inches long and he would have to lay it along the wall, end over end, eighteen times.

Twice it slipped, and twice he had to turn back to the slightly ragged marking of the last sheared baffle blade, scrambling backward and swearing "Sands of Mars!" in a whisper.

The third time the eighteenth measure landed truly. Bigman kept his finger on the spot. Morriss had said the desired place would be almost directly over his head. Bigman turned on his flash, ran his finger along the curved inner surface of the duct, twisted on to his back.

Using his slicer end and holding it, as nearly as he could judge in the dark, some quarter of an inch from actual contact (the force field must not slice in too far), he made a circle with it. Cleaved metal fell on him, and he pushed it to one side.

He turned his flash on the exposed wiring and studied it. Inches farther in would be the interior of a room not a hundred feet from where the man sat at the lock. Was he still sitting there? Obviously, he had not yet pulled the lever (what was he waiting for?) or Bigman would now be very water-logged, very dead. Had he been stopped then, somehow? Taken into custody, perhaps?

A wry grin forced itself onto Bigman's face as he thought that perhaps he was squirming through the interior of a metal worm for nothing.

He was following the wiring. Somewhere here should be a relay. Gently he pulled at the wires, first one, then another. One moved and a small, black, double cone came into view. Bigman sighed his relief. He gripped the flash with his teeth, freeing both hands.

Gingerly, very gingerly, he twisted the two halves of the cone in opposite directions. The magnoclasps yielded, and the two halves moved apart, exposing the contents. They consisted of a break relay: two gleaming contacts, one encased in its field selector and separated from the other by a nearly imperceptible gap. At an appropriate stimulus, such as the pulling of a small lever, the field selector set up the energies that would pull down the other contact, send energy streaming across the point of closure, and open a lock in the dome. It would all happen in a millionth of a second.

Bigman, sweating and half-expecting the final moment to come now, *now,* with his task a second from completion, fumbled in his vest pocket and withdrew a lump of insulating plastic. It was already soft from the warmth of his body. He kneaded it a moment and then brought it down delicately upon the point where the two contacts nearly met. He held it there while he counted three, then withdrew it.

The contacts might close now, but between them there would be a thin film of this plastic, and through it the flow of current could not pass.

The lever could be pulled now: the lock would not open.

Laughing, Bigman scrambled backward, made his way over the remnants of the baffle, passed the struts he had cut away, slid down the slopes. . . .

Bigman searched desperately for Lucky through the confusion that now flooded all the city. The man at the lever was in custody, the transite barrier had been lifted, and the population was flooding back (angry, for the most part, at the city administration for allowing the whole thing to happen) into the homes they had abandoned. To the crowds who had so ghoulishly waited for disaster, the removal of fear was the signal for a high holiday.

At the end Morriss appeared from nowhere and placed a hand on Bigman's sleeve. "Lucky's calling."

Bigman, startled, said, "Where from?"

"From my room in the Council offices. I've told him what you've done."

Bigman flushed with pleasure. Lucky would be proud! He said, "I want to talk to him."

But Lucky's face on the screen was grim. He said, "Congratulations, Bigman, I hear you were terrific."

"It was nothing," grinned Bigman. "But where've you been?"

Lucky said, "Is Dr. Morriss there? I don't see him."

Morriss squeezed his face into the viewer. "Here I am."

"You've captured the man at the lever, according to the news I hear."

"We did. We absolutely did, thanks to Bigman," said Morriss.

"Then let me make a guess. When you closed in on him, he did not try to pull the lever. He simply gave himself up."

"Yes," said Morriss, frowning. "But what makes you guess that?"

"Because the whole incident at the lock was a smoke screen. The real damage was slated to happen at this end. When I realized that, I left. I tried to come back here. I had to use a hopper to get through the crowd and a groundcar the rest of the way."

"And?" asked Morriss anxiously.

"And I was too late!" said Lucky.

Chapter 7

QUESTIONS

THE DAY WAS OVER. The crowd had dispersed. The city had taken on a quiet, almost sleepy atmosphere, with only an occasional knot of two or three still discussing the events of the past several hours.

And Bigman was annoyed.

With Morriss he had left the scene of the recent danger and zoomed out to Council headquarters. There Morriss had had his conference with Lucky, a conference to which Bigman was not allowed entry and from which the Venusian had emerged looking grimly angry. Lucky remained calm but uncommunicative.

Even when they were alone again, Lucky said merely, "Let's get back to the hotel. I need sleep, and so do you after your own little game today."

He hummed the Council March under his breath, as he always did when he was completely abstracted, and signaled a passing tollcar. The car stopped automatically when the sight of his outstretched hand with fingers spread wide registered on its photoelectric scanners.

Lucky pushed Bigman in before him. He turned the dials to indicate the co-ordinate position of the Hotel Bellevue-Aphrodite, put in the proper combination of coins, and let the machine's computer take over. With his foot he adjusted the speed lever to low.

The tollcar drifted forward with a pleasantly smooth motion. Bigman would have found it both comforting and restful if he had been in a less itchingly curious state of mind.

The little Martian flicked a glance at his large friend. Lucky seemed interested only in rest and thought. At least he leaned back on the upholstery and closed his eyes, letting the motion rock him while the hotel seemed to approach and then become a large mouth, which swallowed them as the tollcar automatically found the entrance to the receiving dock of the hotel's garage.

Only when they were in their own room did Bigman reach the point of explosion. He cried, "Lucky, what's it all about? I'm going nuts trying to figure it out."

Lucky stripped off his shirt and said, "Actually, it's only a matter of logic. What kind of accidents occurred as a result of men's being mentally dominated before today? What kind did Morriss mention? A man giving away money. A man dropping a bale of weed. A man placing poison in a nutrient mixture for yeast. In each case, the action was a small one, but it was an *action*. It was something *done*."

"Well?" said Bigman.

"All right, what did we have today? It wasn't something small at all; it was something big. But it wasn't action. It was exactly the opposite of action: A man put his hand on a dome-lock lever and then did nothing. Nothing!"

Lucky vanished into the bathroom and Bigman could hear the needle shower and Lucky's muffled gasps under its invigorating jets. Bigman followed at last, muttering savagely under his breath.

"Hey," he yelled.

Lucky, his muscled body drying in churning puffs of warm air, said, "Don't you get it?"

"Space, Lucky, don't be mysterious, will you? You know I hate that."

"But there's nothing mysterious. The mentalists have changed their entire style, and there must be a reason.

Don't you see the reason for having a man sit at a dome-lock lever and do nothing?"

"I said I didn't."

"Well, what *was* accomplished by it?"

"Nothing."

"Nothing? Great galaxy! Nothing? They only get half the population of Aphrodite and practically every official out to the threatened sector in double-speed time. They get me out there and you and Morriss. Most of the city was left bare, including Council headquarters. And I was such a lunk that it was only when Turner, the city's chief engineer, mentioned how easy it would be to get out of the city with the police force disrupted that it occurred to me what was happening."

"I still don't see it. So help me, Lucky, I'm going to——"

"Hold it, boy," Lucky seized Bigman's threatening fists in one large palm. "Here it is: I got back to Council headquarters as fast as possible and found that Lou Evans had already gone."

"Where did they take him?"

"If you mean the Council, they didn't take him anywhere. He escaped. He knocked down a guard, seized a weapon, used his Council wrist-mark to get a subship and escaped to sea."

"Was *that* what they were really after?"

"Obviously. The threat to the city was strictly a feint. As soon as Evans was safely out into the ocean, the man at the lock was released from control and, naturally, he surrendered."

Bigman's mouth worked. "Sands of Mars! All that stuff in the ventilating duct was for nothing. I was fifty kinds of cobbered fool."

"No, Bigman, you weren't," said Lucky, gravely. "You did a good job, a terrific job, and the Council is going to hear about it."

The little Martian flushed, and for a moment pride left no room in him for anything else. Lucky took the opportunity to get into bed.

Then Bigman said, "But Lucky, that means—— I

mean, if Councilman Evans got away by a trick of the mentalists, then he's guilty, isn't he?"

"No," said Lucky vehemently," he *isn't.*"

Bigman waited, but Lucky had nothing more to say on the subject and instinct told Bigman to let the matter die. It was only after he had burrowed into the cool plastex sheets, having undressed and washed in his turn, that he tried again.

"Lucky?"

"Yes, Bigman."

"What do we do next?"

"Go after Lou Evans."

"We do? What about Morriss?"

"I'm in charge of the project now. I had Chief Councilman Conway put that across all the way from Earth."

Bigman nodded in the darkness. That explained why he himself had not been able to attend the conference. Friend though he might be of Lucky Starr a dozen times over, he was not a member of the Council of Science. And, in a situation where Lucky would have to move in over a fellow councilman's head and call in the authority of Earth and central headquarters to back him, non-councilmen were strictly not wanted as witnesses.

But now the old lust for action was beginning to stir in him. It would be into an ocean now, the vastest, most alien ocean on the inner planets. He said excitedly, "How early do we leave?"

"As soon as the ship they're outfitting is ready. Only first we see Turner."

"The engineer? What for?"

"I have the records on the men involved in the various mentalist incidents in the city up to today, and I want to know about the man at the lock dome, too. Turner is the man who's likely to know most about him. But before we see Turner——"

"Yes?"

"Before that, you Martian peanut, we sleep. Now shut up."

Turner's dwelling place turned out to be a rather large apartment house that seemed suited for people high in the administrative scheme of things. Bigman whistled softly when they passed into the lobby, with its paneled walls and trimensional seascapes. Lucky led the way into a trundle and pressed Turner's apartment number.

The trundle lifted them five floors, then took to the horizontal, skittering along on directed force beams and stopping outside the back entrance to Turner's apartment. They stepped out, and the trundle went off with a whirr, disappearing behind a turn in the corridor.

Bigman watched it wonderingly. "Say, I never saw one of those before."

"It's a Venusian invention," said Lucky. "They're introducing them into new apartment houses on Earth now. You can't do anything about the old apartment houses, though, unless you redesign the building to give each apartment a special trundle-served entrance."

Lucky touched the indicator, which promptly turned red. The door opened, and a woman looked out at them. She was slight of build, young and quite pretty, with blue eyes and blond hair drawn softly backward and over her ears in the Venusian fashion.

"Mr. Starr?"

"That's right, Mrs. Turner," said Lucky. He hesitated a trifle over the title; she was almost too young to be a housewife.

But she smiled at them in friendly fashion. "Won't you come in? My husband's expecting you, but he hasn't had more than two hours' sleep and he's not quite——"

They stepped in, and the door closed behind them.

Lucky said, "Sorry to have to trouble you so early, but it's an emergency, and I doubt that we'll bother Mr. Turner long."

"Oh, that's all right. I understand." She stepped fussily about the room, straightening objects that required no straightening.

Bigman looked about curiously. The apartment was

completely feminine—colorful, frilly, almost fragile. Then, embarrassed to find his hostess's eyes upon him, he said clumsily, "It's a very nice place you have here, miss—uh—ma'am."

She dimpled and said, "Thank you. I don't think Lyman is very fond of the way I have it arranged, but he never objects, and I just love little doodads and whatnots. Don't you?"

Lucky spared Bigman the necessity of answering by saying, "Have you and Mr. Turner been living here very long?"

"Just since we got married. Less than a year. It's a darling apartment house, just about the nicest in Aphrodite. It's got completely independent utilities, its own coaster garage, a central communo. It even has chambers underneath. Imagine! Chambers! Not that anyone ever uses them. Even last night. At least I think no one did, but I can't say, because I just slept right through all the excitement. Can you imagine? I didn't even hear about it till Lyman came home."

"Perhaps that was best," said Lucky. "You missed a fright."

"I missed excitement, you mean," she protested. "Everyone in the apartment was out in the thick of it, and I slept. Slept all through it. No one woke me. I think that was terrible."

"What was terrible?" came a new voice, and Lyman Turner stepped into the room. His hair was rumpled; there were creases on his homely face and sleep in his eyes. He had his precious computer under his arm and put it down under the chair when he sat down.

"My missing the excitement," said his young wife. "How are you, Lyman?"

"All right, considering. And never mind missing the excitement. I'm glad you did. . . . Hello, Starr. Sorry to delay you."

"I've only been here a few moments," said Lucky.

Mrs. Turner flew to her husband and pecked quickly at his cheek. "I'd better leave you men alone now."

Turner patted his wife's shoulder, and his eyes followed her affectionately as she left. He said, "Well, gentlemen, sorry you find me as you do, but I've had a rough time of it in the last few hours."

"I quite realize that. What's the situation with the dome now?"

Turner rubbed his eyes. "We're doubling the men at each lock, and we're making the controls a little less self-contained. That rather reverses the engineering trend of the last century. We're running power lines to various spots in the city so that we can shut the power off from a distance just in case any such thing ever happens again. And, of course, we will strengthen the transite barriers shielding the different sections of the city. . . . Does either of you smoke?"

"No," said Lucky, and Bigman shook his head.

Turner said, "Well, would you toss me a smoke from the dispenser, the thing that looks like a fish? That's right. It's one of my wife's notions. There's no holding her back when it comes to getting these ridiculous gadgets, but she enjoys it." He flushed a little. "I haven't been married long, and I still pamper her, I'm afraid."

Lucky looked curiously at the odd fish, carved out of a stonelike, green material, from whose mouth a lighted cigarette had appeared when he pressed its dorsal fin.

Turner seemed to relax as he smoked. His legs crossed, and one foot moved back and forth in slow rhythm over his computer case.

Lucky said, "Anything new on the man who started it all? The man at the lock?"

"He's under observation. A madman, obviously."

"Does he have a record of mental imbalance?"

"Not at all. It was one of the things I checked into. As chief engineer, you know, the dome personnel are under me."

"I know. It's why I came here to you."

"Well, I wish I could help, but the man was just an ordinary employee. He's been on our rolls for some seven months and never gave any trouble before. In fact, he had an excellent record; quiet, unassuming, diligent."

"Only seven months?"

"That's right."

"Is he an engineer?"

"He has a rating as engineer, but actually his work consisted largely of standing guard at the lock. After all, traffic passes in and out of the city. The lock must be opened and closed, bills of lading checked, records kept. There's a lot more to managing the dome than just engineering."

"Did he have any actual engineering experience?"

"Just an elementary college course. This was his first job. He's quite a young man."

Lucky nodded. He said casually, "I understand there have been a whole series of queer accidents in the city lately."

"Have there?" Turner's weary eyes stared at Lucky, and he shrugged. "I rarely get a chance to look at the news-etheric tapes."

The communo buzzed. Turner lifted it and held it to his ear for a moment. "It's for you, Starr."

Lucky nodded. "I left word I'd be here." He took the communo but did not bother to activate the screen or to raise the sound above the ear-contact stage. He said, "Starr at this end."

Then he put it down and stood up. "We'll be going now, Turner."

Turner rose, too. "All right. If I can help you in the future, call on me any time."

"Thank you. Give our respects to your wife, will you?"

Outside the building Bigman said, "What's up?"

"Our ship is ready," said Lucky, flagging down a groundcar.

They got in, and again Bigman broke the silence. "Did you find out anything from Turner?"

"A thing or two," said Lucky curtly.

Bigman stirred uneasily and changed the subject. "I hope we find Evans."

"I hope so, too."

"Sands of Mars, he's in a spot. The more I think of it,

the worse it seems. Guilty or not, it's rough having a request for removal on grounds of corruption sent in by a superior officer."

Lucky's head turned and he looked down at Bigman. "Morriss never sent any report on Evans to central headquarters. I thought you understood that from yesterday's conversation with him."

"He didn't?" said Bigman incredulously. "Then who did?"

"Great Galaxy!" said Lucky. "Surely it's obvious. Lou Evans sent that message himself, using Morriss's name."

Chapter 8

COUNCILMAN PURSUED!

LUCKY HANDLED THE TRIM SUBSEA CRAFT with growing expertness as he learned the touch of the controls and began to get the feel of the sea about them.

The men who had turned the ship over to them had worriedly suggested a course of instruction as to its management, but Lucky had smiled and confined himself to a few questions while Bigman exclaimed with Bigmanian braggadocio, "There isn't anything that moves that Lucky and I can't handle." Braggadocio or not, it was very nearly true.

The ship, named the *Hilda,* drifted now with the engines cut off. It penetrated the inky blackness of the Venusian ocean with smooth ease. They were navigating blind. Not once had the ship's powerful beams been turned on. Radar, instead, plumbed the abyss ahead more delicately and more informatively than light possibly could.

Along with the radar pulses went the selected microwaves designed to attain maximum reflection from the metal alloy that formed the outer hull of a subship. Their range in the hundreds of miles, the microwaves plunged their probing fingers of energy this direction and that, seeking the particular design of metal that would send them careening back in their tracks.

So far, no reflecting message had come back, and the

Hilda settled down in the ooze, half a mile of water above it, and motionless except for a slow rocking with the mighty sway of Venus's globe-girdling oceanic currents.

For the first hour Bigman had been scarcely aware of the microwaves and the object of their search. He had been lost in the spectacle to be seen from the portholes.

Venusian subsea life is phosphorescent, and the black ocean depths were dotted with colored lights thicker than the stars in space, larger, brighter, and most of all, *moving.* Bigman squashed his nose against the thick glass and stared, fascinated.

Some of the life forms were little round splotches, whose movement was a slow ripple. Others were darting lines. Still others were sea ribbons of the type Lucky and Bigman had seen in the Green Room.

Lucky joined him after a while. He said, "If I remember my xenozoology——"

"Your *what?*"

"That's the study of extraterrestrial animals, Bigman. I've just been looking through a book on Venusian life. I left it on your bunk in case you want to look at it."

"Never mind. I'll take it second hand from you."

"All right. We can start with those little objects. I think that represents a school of buttons."

"Buttons?" said Bigman. Then, "Sure, I see what you mean."

There were a whole series of yellow ovals of light moving across the black field visible through the porthole. Each had black markings on it in the form of two short parallel lines. They moved in brief spurts, settled down for a few moments, then moved again. The dozens in view all moved and rested simultaneously, so that Bigman had the queerly swimming sensation that the buttons weren't moving at all, but that every half minute or so the ship itself lurched.

Lucky said, "They're laying eggs, I think." He was silent for a long moment, then said, "Most of these things I can't make out. Wait! That must be a scarlet patch there. See it? The dark red thing with the irregular outline? It feeds on buttons. Watch it."

There was a scurrying among the yellow blotches of light as they became aware of the swooping predator, but a dozen buttons were blotted out by the angry red of the scarlet patch. Then the patch was the only source of light in the porthole's field of vision. On all sides of it, buttons had scattered away.

"The patch is shaped like a large pancake turned down at the edge," said Lucky, "according to the book. It's hardly anything but skin with a small brain in the center. It's only an inch thick. You can tear it through and through in a dozen places without bothering it. See how irregular the one we're watching is? Arrowfish probably chewed it up a bit."

The scarlet patch moved now, drifting out of sight. There was little left where it had been except for one or two faint, dying glimmers of yellow. Little by little, buttons began moving back again.

Lucky said, "The scarlet patch just settles down to the bottom, holding on to the ooze with its edges and digesting and absorbing whatever it covers. There's another species called the orange patch which is a lot more aggressive. It can shoot a jet of water with enough force to stagger a man, even though it's only a foot wide and not much more than paper thin. The big ones are a lot worse."

"How big do they get?" asked Bigman.

"I haven't the slightest idea. The book says there are occasional reports of tremendous monsters—arrowfish a mile long, and patches that can cover Aphrodite City. No authentic cases, though."

"A mile long! I'll *bet* there aren't any authentic cases."

Lucky's eyebrows lifted. "It's not as impossible as all that. These things here are only shallow-water specimens. The Venusian ocean is up to ten miles deep in spots. There's room in it for a lot of things."

Bigman looked at him doubtfully. "Listen, you're trying to sell me a bale of space dust." He turned abruptly and moved away. "I think I'll look at the book after all."

The *Hilda* moved on and took a new position, while the microwaves shot out, searching and searching. Then again it moved. And again. Slowly Lucky was screening the underwater plateau on which the city of Aphrodite stood.

He waited grimly at the instruments. Somewhere down here his friend Lou Evans *must* be. Evans's ship could navigate neither air nor space, nor any ocean depth of more than two miles, so he *must* be confined to the relatively shallow waters of the Aphrodite plateau.

The first answering flash caught his eye even as he repeated the *must* to himself for the second time. The microwave feedback froze the direction finder in place, and the return pip was brightening the entire receiving field.

Bigman's hand was on Lucky's shoulder instantly. "That's it! That's it!"

"Maybe," said Lucky. "And maybe it's some other ship, or maybe it's only a wreck."

"Get its position, Lucky. Sands of Mars, get its position!"

"I'm doing it, boy, and we're moving."

Bigman could feel the acceleration, hear the churning of the propeller.

Lucky leaned closely over the radio transmitter and its unscrambler, and his voice was urgent. "Lou! Lou Evans! Lucky Starr at this end! Acknowledge signals! Lou! Lou Evans!"

Over and over again, the words pushed out along the ether. The returning microwave pip grew brighter as the distance between the two ships grew less.

No answer.

Bigman said, "That ship we're pipping isn't moving, Lucky. Maybe it *is* a wreck. If it were the councilman, he'd either answer or try to get away from us, wouldn't he?"

"Sh!" said Lucky. His words were quiet and urgent as

he spoke into the transmitter: "Lou! There's no point in trying to hide. I know the truth. I know why you sent the message to Earth in Morriss's name asking for your own recall. And I know who you think the enemy is. Lou Evans! Acknowledge——"

The receiver crackled, static-ridden. Sounds came through the unscrambler and turned into intelligible words: "Stay away. If you know that, stay away!"

Lucky grinned his relief. Bigman whooped.

"You've got him," shouted the little Martian.

"We're coming in to get you," said Lucky into the transmitter. "Hold on. We'll lick it, you and I."

Words came back slowly, "You don't—understand——I'm trying to——" Then, almost in a shriek, "For Earth's sake, Lucky, stay away! Don't get any closer!"

No more came through. The *Hilda* bored toward the position of Evans's ship relentlessly. Lucky leaned back, frowning. He murmured, "If he's *that* afraid, why doesn't he run?"

Bigman didn't hear. He was saying jubilantly, "Terrific, Lucky. That was terrific the way you bluffed him into talking."

"I wasn't bluffing, Bigman," said Lucky, grimly. "I know the key fact involved in this whole mess. So would you, if you stopped to think about it."

Bigman said shakily, "What are you getting at?"

"Do you remember when Dr. Morriss and you and I entered the small room to wait for Lou Evans to be brought to us? Do you remember the first thing that happened?"

"No."

"You started laughing. You said I looked queer and deformed without a mustache. And I felt exactly the same way about you. I said so. Remember?"

"Oh, sure. I remember."

"Did it occur to you to wonder why that was? We'd been watching men with mustaches for hours. Why was it that the thought suddenly occurred to both of us at that particular time?"

"I don't know."

"Suppose the thought had occurred to someone else who had telepathic powers. Suppose the sensation of surprise flooded from his mind to ours."

"You mean the mentalist, or one of them, was in the room with us?"

"Wouldn't that explain it?"

"But it's impossible. Dr. Morriss was the only other man—— Lucky! You don't mean Dr. Morriss!"

"Morriss had been staring at us for hours. Why should he be suddenly amazed at our not having mustaches?"

"Well, then, was someone hiding?"

"Not hiding," said Lucky. "There was one other living creature in the room, and it was in plain view."

"No," cried Bigman. "Oh, no." He burst into laughter. "Sands of Mars, you can't mean the V-frog?"

"Why not?" said Lucky calmly. "We're probably the first men without mustaches it ever saw. It was surprised."

"But it's impossible."

"Is it? They're all over the city. People collect them, feed them, love them. Now do they really love V-frogs? Or do the V-frogs inspire love by mental control so as to get themselves fed and taken care of?"

"Space, Lucky!" said Bigman. "There's nothing surprising about people liking them. They're cute. People don't have to be hypnotized into thinking that."

"Did you like them spontaneously, Bigman? Nothing made you?"

"I'm sure nothing *made* me like them. I just liked them."

"You just liked them? Two minutes after you saw your first V-frog, you fed it. Remember that?"

"Nothing wrong with that, is there?"

"Ah, but what did you feed it?"

"What it liked. Peas dipped in axle g——" The little fellow's voice faded out.

"Exactly. That grease *smelled* like axle grease. There was no mistaking what it was. How did you come to dip the pea in it? Do you always feed axle grease to pet animals? Did you ever know any animal that ate axle grease?"

"Sands of Mars!" said Bigman weakly.

"Isn't it obvious that the V-frog wanted some, and that since you were handy it maneuvered you into delivering some—that you weren't quite your own master?"

Bigman muttered, "I never guessed. But it's so clear when you explain it. I feel terrible."

"Why?"

"It's a hateful thing, having an animal's thoughts rolling around inside your head. It seems unsanitary." His puckish little face screwed up in an expression of revulsion.

Lucky said, "Unfortunately, it's worse then unsanitary."

He turned back to the instruments.

The interval between pip and return disclosed the distance between the two ships to be less than half a mile when, with surprising suddenness, the radar screen showed, unmistakably, the shadow of Evans's ship.

Lucky's voice went out over the transmitter. "Evans, you're in sight now. Can you move? Is your ship disabled?"

The answer came back clearly in a voice torn with emotion. "Earth help me, Lucky, I did my best to warn you. You're trapped! Trapped as I'm trapped."

And as though to punctuate the councilman's wail, a blast of force struck the subship *Hilda*, knocking it to one side and jarring its main motors out of commission!

Chapter 9

OUT OF THE DEEP

IN BIGMAN'S MEMORY AFTERWARD, the events of the next hours were as though viewed through the reverse end of a telescope, a faraway nightmare of confused events.

Bigman had been slammed against the wall by the sudden thrust of force. For what seemed long moments, but was probably little more than a second in actuality, he lay spread-eagled and gasping.

Lucky, still at the controls, shouted, "The main generators are out."

Bigman was struggling to his feet against the crazy slope of the deck. "What happened?"

"We were hit. Obviously. But I don't know how badly."

Bigman said, "The lights are on."

"I know. The emergency generators have cut in."

"How about the main drive?"

"I'm not sure. It's what I'm trying to test."

The engines coughed hoarsely somewhere below and behind. The smooth purr was gone, and in its place a consumptive rattle sounded that set Bigman's teeth on edge.

The *Hilda* shook herself, like a hurt animal, and turned upright. The engines died again.

The radio receiver was echoing mournfully, and now

Bigman gathered his senses sufficiently to try to reach it.

"Starr," it said. "Lucky Starr! Evans at this end. Acknowledge signals."

Lucky got there first. "Lucky speaking. What hit us?"

"It doesn't matter," came the tired voice. "It won't bother you any more. It will be satisfied to let you sit here and die. Why didn't you stay away? I asked you to."

"Is your ship disabled, Evans?"

"It's been stalled for twelve hours. No light, no power—just a little juice I can pump into the radio, and that's fading. Air purifiers are smashed, and the air supply is low. So long, Lucky."

"Can you get out?"

"The lock mechanism isn't working. I've got a subsea suit, but if I try to cut my way out, I'll be smashed."

Bigman knew what Lou Evans meant, and he shuddered. Locks on subsea vessels were designed to let water into the interlock chamber slowly, very slowly. To cut a lock open at the bottom of the sea in an attempt to get out of a ship would mean the entry of water under hundreds of tons of pressure. A human being, even inside a steel suit, would be crushed like an empty tin can under a pile driver.

Lucky said, "We can still navigate. I'm coming to get you. We'll join locks."

"Thanks, but why? If you move, you'll be hit again; and even if you aren't, what's the difference whether I die quickly here or a little more slowly in your ship?"

Lucky retorted angrily, "We'll die if we have to, but not one second *earlier* than we have to. Everyone has to die someday; there's no escaping that, but *quitting* isn't compulsory."

He turned to Bigman. "Get down into the engine room and check the damage. I want to know if it can be repaired."

In the engine room, fumbling with the "hot" micropile by means of long-distance manipulators, which luckily were still in order, Bigman could feel the ship inching painfully along the sea bottom and could hear the husky rasping of the motors. Once he heard a distant boom, followed by a groaning rattle through the framework of the *Hilda* as though a large projectile had hit sea bottom a hundred yards away.

He felt the ship stop, the motor noise drop to a hoarse rumble. In imagination, he could see the *Hilda's* lock extension bore out and close in on the other hull, welding itself tightly to it. He could sense the water between the ships being pumped out of that tube between them and, in actual fact, he saw the lights in the engine room dim as the energy drain on the emergency generators rose to dangerous heights. Lou Evans would be able to step from his ship to the *Hilda* through dry air with no need of artificial protection.

Bigman came up to the control room and found Lou Evans with Lucky. His face was drawn and worn under its blond stubble. He managed a shaky smile in Bigman's direction.

Lucky was saying, "Go on, Lou."

Evans said, "It was the wildest hunch at first, Lucky. I followed up each of the men to whom one of these queer accidents had happened. The one thing I could find in common was that each was a V-frog fancier. Everyone on Venus is, more or less, but each one of *these* fellows kept a houseful of the creatures. I didn't quite have the nerve to make a fool of myself advancing the theory without some facts. If I only had. . . . Anyway, I decided to try to trap the V-frogs into exhibiting knowledge of something that existed in my own mind and in as few others as possible."

Lucky said, "And you decided on the yeast data?"

"It was the obvious thing. I had to have something that wasn't general knowledge or how could I be even reasonably sure they got the information from me? Yeast data was ideal. When I couldn't get any legitimately, I stole some. I borrowed one of the V-frogs at headquarters, put it next to my table, and looked over the papers. I even read some of it aloud. When an accident happened in a yeast plant within two days later involving the exact matter I had read about, I was positive the V-frogs were behind the mess. Only——"

"Only?" prompted Lucky.

"Only I hadn't been so smart," said Evans. "I'd let them into my mind. I'd laid down the red carpet and invited them in, and now I couldn't get them out again. Guards came looking for the papers. I was known to have been in the buildings, so a very polite agent was sent to question me. I returned the papers readily and tried to explain. I couldn't."

"You couldn't? What do you mean by that?"

"I *couldn't*. I was physically unable to. The proper words wouldn't come out. I was unable to say a word about the V-frogs. I even kept getting impulses to kill myself, but I fought them down. They couldn't get me to do something that far from my nature. I thought then: If I can only get off Venus, if I can only get far enough away from the V-frogs, I'd break their hold. So I did the one thing I thought would get me instantly recalled. I sent an accusation of corruption against myself and put Morriss's name to it."

"Yes," said Lucky grimly, "that much I had guessed."

"How?" Evans looked startled.

"Morriss told us his side of your story shortly after we got to Aphrodite. He ended by saying that he was preparing his report to central headquarters. He didn't say he had sent one—only that he was preparing one. But a message had been sent; I knew that. Who else besides Morriss knew the Council code and the circumstances of the case? Only you yourself."

Evans nodded and said bitterly, "And instead of calling me home, they sent you. Is that it?"

"I insisted, Lou. I couldn't believe any charge of corruption against you."

Evans buried his head in his hands. "It was the worst thing you could have done, Lucky. When you subethered you were coming, I begged you to stay away, didn't I? I couldn't tell you why. I was physically incapable of that. But the V-frogs must have realized from my thoughts what a terrific character you were. They could read my opinion of your abilities and they set about having you killed."

"And nearly succeeded," murmured Lucky.

"And *will* succeed this time. For that I am heartily sorry, Lucky, but I couldn't help myself. When they paralyzed the man at the dome lock, I was unable to keep myself from following the impulse to escape, to get out to sea. And, of course, you followed. I was the bait and you were the victim. Again, I tried to keep you away, but I couldn't explain, I couldn't explain. . . ."

He drew a deep, shuddering breath. "I can speak about it now, though. They've lifted the block in my mind. I suppose we're not worth the mental energy they have to expend, because we're trapped, because we're as good as dead and they fear us no longer."

Bigman, having listened this far in increasing confusion, said, "Sands of Mars, what's going on? *Why* are we as good as dead?"

Evans, face still hidden in his hands, did not answer.

Lucky, frowning and thoughtful, said, "We're under an orange patch, a king-size orange patch out of the Venusian deeps."

"A patch big enough to cover the ship?"

"A patch two miles in diameter!" said Lucky. "Two miles across. What slapped the ship into almost a smashup and what nearly hit us a second time when we were making our way over to Evans's ship was a jet of water. Just that! A jet of water with the force of a depth blast."

"But how could we get under it without seeing it?"

Lucky said, "Evans guesses that it's under V-frog mental control, and I think he's right. It could dim its fluorescence by contracting the photo cells in its skin. It could raise one edge of its cape to let us in; and now, here we sit."

"And if we move or try to blast our way out, the patch will let us have it again, and a patch never misses."

Lucky thought, then said suddenly, "But a patch *does* miss! It missed us when we were driving the *Hilda* toward your ship and then we were only going at quarter speed." He turned to Bigman, his eyes narrowed. "Bigman, can the main generators be patched?"

Bigman had almost forgotten the engines. He recovered and said, "Oh—— The micropile alignment hasn't been knocked off, so it can be fixed if I can find all the equipment I need."

"How long will it take?"

"Hours, probably."

"Then get to work. I'm getting out into the sea."

Evans looked up, startled, "What do you mean?"

"I'm going after that patch." He was at the sea-suit locker already, checking to make certain the tiny-force-field linings were in order and well powered and that the oxygen cylinders were full.

It was deceptively restful to be out in the absolute dark. Danger seemed far away. Yet Lucky knew well enough that below him was the ocean bottom and that on every other side, up and all around, was a two-mile-wide inverted bowl of rubbery flesh.

His suit's pump jetted water downward, and he rose slowly with his weapon drawn and ready. He could not help but marvel at the subwater blaster he held. Inventive as man was on his home planet of Earth, it seemed that the necessity for adapting to the cruel environment of an alien planet multiplied his ingenuity a hundred-fold.

Once the new continent of America had burst forth into a brilliance that the ancestral European homelands could never duplicate, and now Venus was showing *her* ability to Earth. There were the city domes, for instance. Nowhere on Earth could force fields have been woven into steel so cleverly. The very suit he wore could not resist the tons of water pressure for a moment without the microfields that webbed its interior braces (always provided those tons were introduced sufficiently slowly). In many other respects that suit was a marvel of engineering. Its jet device for underwater traveling, its efficient oxygen supply, its compact controls, were all admirable.

And the weapon he held!

But immediately his thoughts moved to the monster above. That was a Venusian invention, too. An invention of the planet's evolution. Could such things be on Earth? Not on land, certainly. Living tissue couldn't support the weight of more than forty tons against Earth's gravity. The giant brontosauri of Earth's Mesozoic Age had legs like treetrunks, yet had to remain in the marshes so that water could help buoy them up.

That was the answer: water's buoyancy. In the oceans any size of creature might exist. There were the whales of Earth, larger than any dinosaur that ever lived. But this monstrous patch above them must weigh two hundred million *tons*, he calculated. Two million large whales put together would scarcely weigh that. Lucky wondered how old it was. How old would a thing have to be to grow as large as two million whales? A hundred years? A thousand years? Who could tell?

But size could be its undoing, too. Even under the ocean. The larger it grew, the slower its reactions. Nerve impulses took time to travel.

Evans thought the monster refrained from hitting them with another water jet because, having disabled them, it was indifferent to their further fate, or rather the V-frogs who manipulated the giant patch were. That might not be so! It might be rather that the monster needed time to suck its tremendous water sac full. It needed time to aim.

Furthermore, the monster could scarcely be at its best. It was adapted to the deeps, to layers of water six miles or more high above it. Here its efficiency must necessarily be cut down. It had missed the *Hilda* on its second try, probably because it had not fully recovered from the previous stroke.

But now it was waiting; its water sac was slowly filling; and as much as it could in the shallow water surrounding it, it was gathering its strength. He, Lucky, 190 pounds of man against two hundred million tons of monster, would have to stop it.

Lucky looked upward. He could see nothing. He

pressed a contact on the inner lining in the left middle
finger of the sheathed force-field-reinforced mitten that
gauntleted his hand, and a jab of pure-white light
poured out of the metal fingertip. It penetrated upward
hazily and ended in nothingness. Was that the monster's
flesh at the far end? Or just the petering out of the light
beam?

Three times the monster had jetted water. Once and
Evans's ship had been smashed. A second time and
Lucky's ship had been mauled. (But not as badly; was
the creature getting weaker?) A third time, prematurely,
and the stroke had been a miss.

He raised his weapon. It was bulky, with a thick
handgrip. Within that grip was a hundred miles of wire
and a tiny generator that could put out huge voltages.
He pointed it upward and squeezed his fist.

For a moment, nothing—but he knew the hair-thin
wire was squirting out and upward through the carbonated ocean water. . . .

Then it hit and Lucky saw the results. For in the moment that the wire made contact, a flash current of electricity screamed along it at the speed of light and flayed
the obstruction with the force of a bolt of lightning. The
hairlike wire gleamed brilliantly and vaporized steaming
water into murky froth. It was more than steam, for the
alien water writhed and bubbled horribly as the dis-
solved carbon dioxide gassed out. Lucky felt himself
bobbing in the wild currents set up.

Above all that, above the steaming and bubbling,
above the water's churning and the line of thin fire that
reached upward, there was a fireball that exploded.
Where the wire had touched living flesh there was a
blaze of furious energy. It burned a hole ten feet wide
and as many feet deep into the living mountain above
him.

Lucky smiled grimly. That was only a pin prick in
comparison to the monster's vast bulk, but the patch
would feel it; or at least in ten minutes or so, it would
feel it. The nerve impulses must first travel their slow
way along the curve of its flesh. When the pain reached

the creature's tiny brain, it would be distracted from the helpless ship on the ocean floor and turn upon its new tormentor.

But, Lucky thought grimly, the monster would not find him. In ten minutes, he would have changed position. In ten minutes, he——

Lucky never completed the thought. Not one minute after his bolt had struck the creature, it struck back.

Not one minute had passed when Lucky's shocked and tortured senses told him that he was being driven down, down, down, in a turbulent jet of madly driving water. . . .

Chapter 10

THE MOUNTAIN OF FLESH

THE SHOCK SENT LUCKY'S SENSES REELING. Any suit of ordinary metal would have bent and smashed. Any man of ordinary mettle would have been carried senseless down to the ocean floor, there to be smashed into concussion and death.

But Lucky fought desperately. Struggling against the mighty current, he brought his left arm up to his chest to check the dials that indicated the state of the suit machinery.

He groaned. The indicators were all lifeless things, their delicate workings jarred into uselessness. Still, his oxygen supply seemed unaffected (his lungs would have told him of any drop in pressure), and his suit obviously wasn't leaking. He could only hope that its jet action was still in order

There was no use trying blindly to find his way out of the stream by main force. He almost certainly lacked the power. He would have to wait and gamble on one important thing: The stream of water lost velocity rapidly as it penetrated downward. Water against water was a high-friction action. At the rim of the jet, turbulence would grow and eat inward. A cutting stream five hundred feet across as it emerged from the creature's blowpipe might be only fifty feet wide when it hit bottom, depending upon its original velocity and the distance to the ocean floor.

And that original velocity would have slowed, too. That did not mean that the final velocity was anything to deride. Lucky had felt its force against the ship.

It all depended on how far from the center of the water gush he was, on how near a bulls-eye the creature scored.

The longer he waited, the better his chances—provided he did not wait too long. With his metal-gloved hand on the jet controls, Lucky let himself be flung downward, trying to wait calmly, striving to guess how close to solid bottom he was, expecting each moment the one last concussion he would never feel.

And then, when he had counted ten, he flung his suit's jets open. The small, high-speed propellers on either shoulder blade ground in harsh vibration as they threw out water at right angles to the main current. Lucky could feel his body take on a new direction of fall.

If he was dead center, it wouldn't help. The energy he could pump up would not suffice to overcome the mighty surge downward. If he was well off center, however, his velocity would, by now, have slowed considerably and the growing zone of turbulence might not be far off.

And as he thought that, he felt his body bob and yank with nauseating violence, and he knew he was safe.

He kept his own jets in operation, turning their force downward now and, as he did so, he turned his finger light in the direction of the ocean floor. He was just in time to see the ooze, some fifty feet below, explode and obscure everything with its muck.

He had made his way out of the stream with but seconds to spare.

He was hurrying upward now, as fast as the jet motors of his suit would carry him. He was in desperate haste. In the darkness within his helmet (darkness within darkness within darkness) his lips were pressed into a narrow line and his eyebrows pulled down low.

He was doing his best not to think. He had thought

enough in those few seconds in the water spout. He had underestimated the enemy. He had assumed it was the gigantic patch that was aiming at him, and it wasn't. It was the V-frogs on the water's surface that controlled the patch's body through its mind! The V-frogs had aimed. They did not have to follow the patch's sensations in order to know it had been hit. They needed only to read Lucky's mind, and they needed only to aim at the source of Lucky's thoughts.

So it was no longer a matter of pin-pricking the monster into moving away from the *Hilda* and lumbering down the long underwater declivity to the deeps that had spawned it. The monster had to be killed outright.

And quickly!

If the *Hilda* would not take another direct blow, neither would Lucky's own suit. The indicators were gone already; the controls might go next. Or the liquid-oxygen containers might suffer damage to their tiny force-field generators.

Up and still up went Lucky, up to the only place of safety. Although he had never seen the monster's blow-pipe, it stood to reason that it must be an extensible and flexible tube that could point this way and that. But the monster could scarcely point it at its own undersurface. For one thing, it would do itself damage. For another, the force of the water it expelled would prevent that blowpipe from bending at so great an angle.

Lucky had to move up then, close to the animal's undersurface, to where its weapon of water could not reach; and he had to do it before the monster could fill its water sac for another blow.

Lucky flashed his light upward. He was reluctant to do so, feeling instinctively that the light would make him an easy target. His mind told him his instinct was wrong. The sense that was responsible for the monster's rapid response to his attack was not sight.

Fifty feet or less above, the light ended on a rough, grayish surface, streaked with deep corrugations. Lucky scarcely attempted to brake his rush. The monster's skin was rubbery and his own suit hard. Even as he thought that, he collided, pressing upward and feeling the alien flesh give.

For a long moment, Lucky drew deep gasps of relief. For the first time since leaving the ship, he felt moderately safe. The relaxation did not last, however. At any time the creature could turn its attack (or the small mind-master that controlled it could) on the ship. That must not be allowed to happen.

Lucky played his finger flash about his surroundings with a mixture of wonder and nausea.

Here and there in the undersurface of the monster were holes some six feet across into which, as Lucky could see by the flow of bubbles and solid particles, water was rushing. At greater intervals were slits, which opened occasionally into ten-foot-long fissures that emitted frothing gushes of water.

Apparently this was the way the monster fed. It poured digestive juices into the portion of the ocean trapped beneath its bulk, then sucked in water by the cubic yard to extract the nutriment it contained, and still later expelled water, debris, and its own wastes.

Obviously, it could not stay too long over any one spot of the ocean or the accumulation of its own waste products would make its environment unhealthy. Of its own account it would not have lingered here so long, but with the V-frogs driving it——

Lucky moved jerkily through no action of his own and, in surprise, turned the beam of light on a spot closer to himself. In a moment of stricken horror, he realized the purposes of those deep corrugations he had noticed in the monster's undersurface. One such was forming directly to one side of him and was sucking inward, into the creature's substance. The two sides of the corrugation rubbed against one another, and the whole was obviously a grinding mechanism whereby the monster broke up and shredded particles of food too large to be handled directly by its intake pores.

Lucky did not wait. He could not risk his battered suit against the fantastic strength of the monster's muscles. The walls of his suit might hold, but portions of the delicate working mechanisms might not.

He swung his shoulder so as to turn the suit's jets directly against the flesh of the monster and gave them full energy. He came loose with a sharp smacking sound, then veered round and back.

He did not touch the skin again, but hovered near it and traveled along it, following the direction against gravity, mounting upward, away from the outer edges of the thing, toward its center.

He came suddenly to a point where the creature's undersurface turned down again in a wall of flesh that extended as far as his light would reach on either side. That wall quivered and was obviously composed of thinner tissue.

It was the blowpipe.

Lucky was sure that was what it was—a gigantic cavern a hundred yards across, out of which the fury of rushing water emerged. Cautiously Lucky circled it. Undoubtedly this was the safest place one could be, here at the very base of the blowpipe, and yet he picked his way gingerly.

He knew what he was looking for, however, and he left the blowpipe. He moved away in the direction in which the monster's flesh mounted still higher, until he was at the peak of the inverted bowl, and there it was!

At first, Lucky was aware only of a long-drawn-out rumble, almost too deep to hear. In fact, it was vibration that attracted his attention, rather than any sound. Then he spied the swelling in the monster's flesh. It writhed and beat; a huge mass, hanging thirty feet downward and perhaps as big around as the blowpipe.

That *must* be the center of the organism; its heart, or whatever passed for its heart, must be there. That heart must beat in powerful strokes, and Lucky felt dizzy as he tried to picture it. Those heartbeats must last five minutes at a time, during which thousands of cubic yards of blood (or whatever the creature used) must be forced through blood vessels large enough to hold the

Hilda. That heartbeat must suffice to drive the blood a mile and back.

What a mechanism it must be, thought Lucky. If one could only capture such a thing alive and study its physiology!

Somewhere in that swelling must also be what brain the monster might have. Brain? Perhaps what passed for its brain was only a small clot of nerve cells without which the monster could live quite well.

Perhaps! But it couldn't live without its heart. The heart had completed one beat. The central swelling had contracted to almost nothing. Now the heart was relaxing for another beat five minutes or more from now, and the swelling was expanding and dilating as blood rushed into it.

Lucky raised his weapon and with his light beam full on that giant heart, he let himself sink down. It might be best not to be too close. On the other hand, he dared not miss.

For a moment a twinge of regret swept him. From a scientific standpoint it was almost a crime to kill this mightiest of nature's creatures.

Was that one of his own thoughts or a thought imposed upon him by the V-frogs on the ocean surface?

He dared wait no longer. He squeezed the handgrip of his weapon. The wire shot out. It made contact, and Lucky's eyes were blinded by the flash of light in which the near wall of the monster's heart was burnt through.

For minutes the water boiled with the death throes of the mountain of flesh. Its entire mass convulsed in its gigantic writhings. Lucky, thrown this way and that, was helpless.

He tried to call the *Hilda,* but the answer consisted of erratic gasps, and it was quite obvious that the ship, too, was being flung madly about.

But death, when it comes, must finally penetrate the last ounce of even a hundred-million-ton life. Eventually a stillness came upon the water.

And Lucky moved downward slowly, slowly, weary nearly to death.

He called the *Hilda* again. "It's dead," he said. "Send out the directional pulse and let me follow it down."

Lucky let Bigman remove his sea suit and managed a smile as the little Martian looked worriedly up at him.

"I never thought I'd see you again, Lucky," said Bigman, gulping noisily.

"If you're going to cry," said Lucky, "turn your head away. I didn't get in out of the ocean just to get all wet in here. How are the main generators coming along?"

"They'll be all right," put in Evans, "but it will still take time. The knocking around just at the end there ruined one of the welding jobs."

"Well," said Lucky, "we'll just have to get on with it." He sat down with a weary sigh. "Things didn't go quite as I expected."

"In what way?" demanded Evans.

"It was my notion," said Lucky, "to pin-prick the monster into moving off us. That didn't work, and I had to kill him. The result is that its dead body has settled down around the *Hilda* like a collapsed tent."

Chapter 11

TO THE SURFACE?

"YOU MEAN WE'RE TRAPPED?" said Bigman, with horror.

"You can put it that way," said Lucky coolly. "You can also say that we're safe, if you want to. Certainly we're safer here than anywhere on Venus. Nobody can do anything to us physically with that mountain of dead meat over us. And when the generators are repaired, we'll just force our way out. Bigman, get at those generators; and Evans, let's pour ourselves some coffee and talk this thing over. There might not be another chance for a quiet chat."

Lucky welcomed this respite, this moment when there was nothing to be done but talk and think.

Evans, however, was upset. His china-blue eyes crinkled at the corners.

Lucky said, "You look worried?"

"I am worried. What in space and time do we do?"

Lucky said, "I've been thinking about that. It seems to me that all we can do is get the V-frog story to someone who's safe from any mental control by them."

"And who's that?"

"No one on Venus. That's for sure."

Evans stared at his friend. "Are you trying to tell me that everyone on Venus is under control?"

"No, but anyone *might* be. After all, there are different ways in which the human mind can be manipulated by these creatures." Lucky rested one arm over the back of the pilot swivel and crossed his legs. "In the first place, complete control can be taken for a short period of time over a man's mind. *Complete* control! During that interval a human being can be made to do things contrary to his own nature, things that endanger his own life and others': the pilots on the coaster, for instance, when Bigman and I first landed on Venus."

Evans said grimly, "That type of thing hasn't been *my* trouble."

"I know. That's what Morriss failed to realize. He was sure you weren't under control simply because you showed no signs of amnesia. But there's a second type of control that you suffered from. It's less intense, so a person retains his memory. However, just because it's less intense, a person cannot be forced to do anything against his own nature; you couldn't be forced to commit suicide, for instance. Still, the power lasts longer—days rather than hours. The V-frogs make up in time what they lose in intensity. Well, there must be still a third kind of control."

"And that is?"

"A control that is still less intense than the second type. A control that is so mild the victim isn't even aware of it, yet strong enough so that the victim's mind can be rifled and picked of its information. For instance, there's Lyman Turner."

"The chief engineer on Aphrodite?"

"That's right. He's a case in point. Can you see that? Consider that there was a man at the dome lock yesterday who sat there with a lever in his hand, endangering the whole city, yet he was so tightly protected all around, so netted about with alarms that no one could approach him without warning until Bigman forced a passage through a ventilator shaft. Isn't that odd?"

"No. Why is it odd?"

"The man had only been on the job a matter of months He wasn't even a real engineer. His work was

more like that of a clerk or an office boy. Where did
he get the information to protect himself so? How could
he possibly know the force and power system in that
section of the dome so thoroughly?"

Evans pursed his lips and whistled soundlessly. "Hey,
that *is* a point."

"The point didn't strike Turner. I interviewed him on
just that matter before getting on the *Hilda*. I didn't
tell him what I was after, of course. He himself told
me about the fellow's inexperience, but the incongruity
of the matter never struck him. Yet who *would* have
the necessary information? Who but the chief engineer?
Who better than he?"

"Right. Right."

"Well, then, suppose Turner was under very gentle
control. The information could be lifted out of his
brain. He could be very gently soothed into not seeing
anything out of the way in the situation. Do you see
what I mean? And then Morriss——"

"Morriss, too?" said Evans, shocked.

"Possibly, He's convinced it's a matter of Sirians
after yeast. He can see it as nothing else. Is that a legit-
imate misjudgment or is he being subtly persuaded?
He was ready to suspect you, Lou—a little too ready.
One councilman ought to be a little less prepared to
suspect another."

"Space! Then who's safe, Lucky?"

Lucky stared at his empty coffee cup and said, "No
one on Venus. That's my point. We've got to get the
story and the truth somewhere else."

"And how can we?"

"A good point. How can we?" Lucky Starr brooded
over that.

Evans said, "We can't leave physically. The *Hilda*
is designed for nothing but ocean. It can't navigate the
air, let alone space. And if we go back to the city to
get something more suitable, we'd never leave it again."

"I think you're right," said Lucky, "but we don't
have to leave Venus in the flesh. Our information is
all that has to leave."

"If you mean ship's radio," said Evans, "that's out, too. The set we've got on this tub is strictly intra-Venus. It's not a subetheric, so it can't reach Earth. Down here, as a matter of fact, the instrument won't reach above the ocean. Its carrier waves are designed to be reflected down from the ocean surface so that they can get distance. Besides that, even if we could transmit straight up, we couldn't reach Earth."

"I don't see that we have to," said Lucky. "There's something between here and Earth that would do just as well."

For a moment, Evans was mystified. Then he said, "You mean the space stations?"

"Surely. Two space stations circle Venus. Earth may be anywhere from thirty to fifty million miles away, but the stations may be as close as two thousand miles to this point. Yet there can't be V-frogs on the stations, I'm sure. Morriss said they dislike free oxygen, and one could scarcely rig up special carbon-dioxide chambers for V-frogs considering the economy with which space stations must be run. Now, if we could get a message out to the stations for relay to central headquarters on Earth, we'd have it."

"That's it, Lucky," said Evans, excitedly. "It's our way out. Their mental powers can't possibly reach two thousand miles across space to——" But then his face turned glum once more. "No, it won't do. The subship radio still can't reach past the ocean surface."

"Maybe not from here. But suppose we go up to the surface and transmit from there directly into the atmosphere."

"Up to the surface?"

"Well?"

"But *they* are there. The V-frogs."

"I know that."

"We'll be put under control."

"Will we?" said Lucky. "So far they've never tackled anyone who's known about them, known what to expect and made up his mind to resist it. Most of the victims were completely unsuspecting. In your case you actually invited them into your mind, to use your own phrase. Now I am not unsuspecting, and I don't propose to issue any invitations."

"You can't do it, I tell you. You don't know what it's like."

"Can you suggest an alternative?"

Before Evans could answer, Bigman entered, rolling down his sleeves. "All set," he said. "I guarantee the generators."

Lucky nodded and stepped to the controls, while Evans remained in his seat, his eyes clouded with uncertainty.

There was the churning of the motors again, rich and sweet. The muted sound was like a song, and there was that strange feeling of suspension and motion under one's feet that was never felt on a spaceship.

The *Hilda* moved through the bubble of water that had been trapped under the collapsing body of the giant patch and built up speed.

Bigman said uneasily, "How much room do we have?"

"About half a mile," said Lucky.

"What if we don't make it?" muttered Bigman. "What if we just hit it and stick, like an ax in a tree stump?"

"Then we pull out and try again," said Lucky.

There was silence for a moment, and Evans said in a low voice, "Being closed in under here, under the patch —it's like being in a chamber." He was mumbling, half to himself.

"In a what?" said Lucky.

"In a chamber," said Evans, still abstracted. "They build them on Venus. They're little transite domes under sea-floor level, like cyclone cellars or bomb shelters on Earth. They're supposed to be protection against incoming water in case of a broken dome, say by Venusquake. I don't know that a chamber has ever been used, but the better apartment houses always advertise that they have chamber facilities in case of emergency."

Lucky listened to him, but said nothing.

The engine pitch rose higher.

"Hold on!" said Lucky.

Every inch of the *Hilda* trembled, and the sudden, almost irresistible deceleration forced Lucky hard against the instrument panel. Bigman's and Evans's knuckles went white and their wrists strained as they gripped the guard rails with all their strength.

The ship slowed but did not stop. With the motors straining and the generators protesting in a squeal that made Lucky wince in sympathy, the *Hilda* plowed through skin and flesh and sinew, through empty blood-vessels and useless nerves that must have resembled two-foot-thick cables. Lucky, jaw set and grim, kept the drive rod nailed at maximum against the tearing resistance.

The long minutes passed and then, in a long churn of triumphant engine, they were through—through the monster and out once more into the open sea.

Silently and smoothly the *Hilda* rose through the murky, carbon-dioxide-saturated water of Venus's ocean. Silence held the three, a silence that seemed enforced by the daring with which they were storming the very fortress of Venus's hostile life form. Evans had not said a word since the patch had been left behind. Lucky had locked ship's controls and now sat on the pilot swivel with fingers softly tapping his knee. Even the irrepressible Bigman had drifted glumly to the rear port with its bellying, wide-angle field of vision.

Suddenly Bigman called, "Lucky, look there."

Lucky strode to Bigman's side. Together they gazed in silence. Over half the field of the port there was only the starry light of small phosphorescent creatures, thick and soft, but in another direction there was a wall, a monstrous wall glowing in smears of shifting color.

"Do you suppose that's the patch, Lucky?" asked Bigman. "It wasn't shining that way when we came down here; and anyway, it wouldn't shine after it was dead, would it?"

Lucky said thoughtfully, "It is the patch in a way, Bigman. I think the whole ocean is gathering for the feast."

Bigman looked again and felt a little ill. Of course! There were hundreds of millions of tons of meat there for the taking, and the light they viewed must be the light of all the small creatures of the shallows feeding on the dead monster.

Creatures darted past the port, moving always in the same direction. They moved sternward, toward the mountainous carcass the *Hilda* had left behind.

Pre-eminent among them were arrow fish of all sizes. Each had a straight white line of phosphorescence that marked its backbone (it wasn't a backbone really, but merely an unjointed rod of horny substance). At one end of that white line was a pale yellow V that marked the head. To Bigman it looked indeed as though a countless swarm of animated arrows were swarming past the ship, but in imagination he could see their needle-rimmed jaws, cavernous and ravenous.

"Great Galaxy!" said Lucky.

"Sands of Mars!" murmured Bigman. "The ocean will be empty. Every blasted thing in the ocean is gathering to this one spot."

Lucky said, "At the rate those arrow fish must be gorging themselves, the thing will be gone in twelve hours."

Evans's voice sounded from behind them. "Lucky, I want to speak to you."

Lucky turned. "Sure. What is it, Lou?"

"When you first suggested going to the surface, you asked if I could propose an alternative."

"I know. You didn't answer."

"I can answer now. I'm holding it, in fact, and the answer is that we're going back to the city."

Bigman called, "Hey, what's the idea?"

Lucky had no need to ask that question. His nostrils flared, and inwardly he raged at himself for those minutes he had spent at the porthole when all his heart, mind, and soul should have been concentrated on the business at hand.

For in Evans's clenched fist, as it lifted from his side, was Lucky's own blaster, and in Evans's narrowed eyes, there was hard determination.

"We're going back to the city," repeated Evans.

Chapter 12

TO THE CITY?

LUCKY SAID, "WHAT'S WRONG, LOU?"

Evans gestured impatiently with his blaster. "Put the engines in reverse, start bottomward, and turn the ship's bow toward the city. Not you, Lucky. You let Bigman go to those controls; then you get in line with him, so I can watch both of you and the controls, too."

Bigman had his hands half-upraised, and his eyes turned to look at Lucky. Lucky kept his hands at his side.

Lucky said flatly, "Suppose you tell me what's biting you?"

"Nothing's biting me," said Evans. "Nothing at all. It's what's biting you. You went out and killed the monster, then came back and started talking about going to the surface. Why?"

"I explained my reasons."

"I don't believe your reasons. If we surface, I know the V-frogs will take over our minds. I've had experience with them, and because of that I know the V-frogs have taken over *your* mind."

"*What?*" exploded Bigman. "Are you nuts?"

"I know what I'm doing," said Evans, watching Lucky warily. "If you look at this thing coolly, Bigman, you'll see that Lucky must be under V-frog influence. Don't forget, he's my friend, too. I've known him longer than you have, Bigman, and it bothers me to have to do this, but there's no way out. It must be done."

Bigman stared uncertainly at both men, then said in a low voice, "Lucky, have the V-frogs really got you?"

"No," said Lucky.

"What do you expect him to say?" demanded Evans with heat. "Of course they have him. To kill the monster, he had to jet upward to its top. He must have gone fairly close to the surface where the V-frogs were waiting, close enough for them to snatch him. They let him kill the monster. Why not? They would be glad to trade control of the monster for control of Lucky, so Lucky came back babbling of the need to go to the surface, where we'll all be among them, all trapped—the only men who know the truth helpless."

"Lucky?" quavered Bigman, his tone pleading for reassurance.

Lucky Starr said calmly, "You're quite wrong, Lou. What you're doing now is only the result of your own captivity. You've been under control before, and the V-frogs know your mind. They can enter it at will. Maybe they've never entirely left it. You're doing only what you're being made to do."

Evans's grip on his blaster hardened. "Sorry, Lucky, but it won't do. Let's get the ship back to the city."

Lucky said, "If you're not under control, Lou—if you're mind-free—then you'll blast me down if I try to force us up to the surface, won't you?"

Evans did not answer.

Lucky said, "You'll have to. It will be your duty to the Council and to Mankind to do so. On the other hand, if you are under mental control, you may be forced to threaten me, to try to make me change ship's course, but I doubt that you can be forced to kill me. Actually murdering a friend and fellow councilman would be too much against your basic ways of thought. —So give me your blaster."

Lucky advanced toward the other, hand outstretched. Bigman stared in horror.

Evans backed away. He said hoarsely, "I'm warning you, Lucky. I'll shoot."

"I say you won't shoot. You'll give me the blaster."

Evans was back against the wall. His voice rose crazily. "I'll shoot. I'll shoot!"

Bigman cried, "Lucky, stop!"

But Lucky had already stopped and was backing away. Slowly, very slowly, he backed.

The life had suddenly gone out of Evans's eyes, and he was standing now, a carved stone image, finger firm on trigger. Evans's voice was cold. "Back to the city."

Lucky said, "Get the ship on the city course, Bigman."

Bigman stepped quickly to the controls. He muttered, "He's really under now, isn't he?"

Lucky said, "I was afraid it might happen. They've shifted him to intense control to make sure he shoots. And he will, too; no question about it. He's in amnesia now. He won't remember this part afterward."

"Can he hear us?" Bigman remembered the pilots on the coaster in which they had landed on Venus and their apparent complete disregard of the external world about them.

"I don't think so," said Lucky, "but he's watching the controls and if we deviate from city-direction, he'll shoot. Make no mistake about that."

"Then what do we do?"

Words again issued from between Evans's pale, cold lips: "Back to the city. Quickly!"

Lucky, motionless, eyes fixed on the unwavering muzzle of his friend's blaster, spoke softly and quickly to Bigman.

Bigman acknowledged the words by the slightest of nods.

The *Hilda* moved back along the path it had come, back toward the city.

Lou Evans, councilman, stood against the wall, white-faced and stern, his pitiless eyes shifting from Lucky to Bigman to the controls. His body, frozen into utter obedience to those who controlled his mind, did not even feel the need of shifting the blaster from one hand to the other.

Lucky strained his ears to hear the low sound of Aphrodite's carrier beam as it sounded steadily on the *Hilda's* direction finder. The beam radiated in all directions on a definite wave length from the topmost point of Aphrodite's dome. The route back to the city became as obvious as though Aphrodite were in plain sight and a hundred feet away.

Lucky could tell by the exact pitch of the beam's low whine that they were not approaching the city directly. It was a small difference indeed, and one that was not at all obvious to the ear. To Evans's controlled ears, it might pass unnoticed. Fervently, Lucky hoped so.

Lucky tried to follow Evans's blank glare when his eyes rested on the controls. He was certain that it was the depth indicator that those eyes rested upon. It was a large dial, a simple one that measured the water pressure. At the distance Evans stood it was simple enough to tell that the *Hilda* was not nosing surfaceward.

Lucky felt certain that, should the depth-indicator needle vary in the wrong direction, Evans would blast without a moment's hesitation.

Try as he might to think as little as possible about the situation, to allow as few specific thoughts as possible to be picked up by the waiting V-frogs, he could not help but wonder why Evans did not shoot them out of hand. They had been marked for death under the giant patch, but now they were only being herded back to Aphrodite.

Or would Evans shoot them down just as soon as the V-frogs could overcome some last scruple in the captive's subjected mind?

The carrier beam moved a little further off pitch. Again Lucky's eyes flickered quickly in Evans's direction. Was he imagining it, or did a spark of something (not emotion, exactly, but something) show in Evans's eyes?

A split second later it was obviously more than

imagination, for there was a definite tightening of Evans's biceps, a small lifting of his arm.

He was going to shoot!

And even as the thought passed quickly through Lucky's mind and his muscles tensed involuntarily and uselessly for the coming of the blast, the ship crashed. Evans, caught unaware, toppled backward. The blaster slithered from his sprawling fingers.

Lucky acted instantly. The same shock that threw Evans back threw him forward. He rode that shock and came down upon the other, clutching for his wrist and seizing it with steely fingers.

But Evans was anything but a pigmy, and he fought with the unearthly rage that was imposed upon him. He doubled his knees above him, caught Lucky in the thighs, and heaved. The still rocking ship fortuitously added its roll to the force of Evans's thrust and the captive councilman was on top.

Evans's fist pounded, but Lucky's shoulder fended the blow. He raised his own knees and caught Evans in an iron scissors hold just below the hips.

Evans's face distorted with pain. He twisted, but Lucky writhed with him and was on top once more. He sat up, his legs maintaining their hold, increasing it.

Lucky said, "I don't know if you can hear or understand me, Lou——"

Evans paid no regard. With one last contortion of his body, he flung himself and Lucky into the air, breaking Lucky's hold.

Lucky rolled as he hit the floor and came lithely to his feet. He caught Evans's arm as the latter rose and swung it over his shoulder. A heave and Evans came crashing down on his back. He lay still.

"Bigman!" said Lucky, breathing quickly and brushing back his hair with a quick motion of his hand.

"Here I am," said the little fellow, grinning and swinging Turner's blaster lightly. "I was all set, just in case."

"All right. Put that blaster away, Bigman, and look

Lou over. Make sure there are no bones broken. Then tie him up."

Lucky was at the controls now, and with infinite caution he backed the *Hilda* off the remnants of the carcass of the giant patch he had killed hours before.

Lucky's gamble had worked. He had hoped that the V-frogs with their preoccupation with mentalities would have no real conception of the physical size of the patch, that with their lack of experience of subsea travel, they would not realize the significance of the slight off-course route Bigman had taken. The whole gamble had been in the quick phrase which Lucky had spoken to Bigman as the latter had turned the ship back to the city under the threat of Evans's blaster.

"Afoul of the patch," he had said.

Again the *Hilda's* course changed. Its nose lifted upward.

Evans, bound to his bunk, stared with weary shamefacedness at Lucky. "Sorry."

"We understand, Lou. Don't brood about it," said Lucky lightly. "But we can't let you go for a while. You see that, don't you?"

"Sure. Space, put more knots on me. I deserve it. Believe me, Lucky, most of it I don't even remember."

"Look, you better get some sleep, fella," and Lucky's fist punched Evans lightly in the shoulder. "We'll wake you when we hit surface, if we have to."

To Bigman, a few minutes later, he said quietly, "Round up every blaster on the ship, Bigman, every weapon of every sort. Look through stores, the bunk lockers, everywhere."

"What are you going to do?"

"Dump them," said Lucky succinctly.

"What?"

"You heard me. You might go under. Or I might. If we do, I don't want anything with which we can expect a repetition of what has just happened. Against the V-frogs, physical weapons are useless, anyway."

One by one, two blasters, plus the electric whips from

each sea suit, passed through the trash ejector. The ejector's hinged opening stood flush with the wall just next to the first-aid cupboard, and through it the weapons were puffed through one-way valves into the sea.

"It makes me feel naked," muttered Bigman, staring out through the port as though to catch sight of the vanished weapons. A dim phosphorescent streak flashed across, marking the passing of an arrow fish. That was all.

The water pressure needle dropped slowly. They had been twenty-eight hundred feet under to begin with. They were less than two thousand now.

Bigman continued peering intently out the port.

Lucky glanced at him. "What are you looking for?"

"I thought," said Bigman, "it would get lighter as we got up toward the top."

"I doubt it," said Lucky. "The seaweed blankets the surface tightly. It will stay black till we break through."

"Think we might meet up with a trawler, Lucky?"

"I hope not."

They were fifteen hundred feet under now.

Bigman said with an effort at lightness, a visible attempt to change the current of his own thoughts, "Say, Lucky, how come there's so much carbon dioxide in the air on Venus? I mean, with all these plants? Plants are supposed to turn carbon dioxide into oxygen, aren't they?"

"On Earth they are. However, if I remember my course in xenobotany, Venusian plant life has a trick all its own. Earth plants liberate their oxygen into the air; Venusian plants store theirs as high-oxygen compounds in their tissues." He talked absently as though he himself was also using speech as a guard against too-deep thinking. "That's why no Venusian animal breathes. They get all the oxygen they need in their food."

"What do you know?" said Bigman in astonishment.

"In fact, their food probably has too much oxygen for them, or they wouldn't be so fond of low-oxygen food, like the axle grease you fed the V-frog. At least, that's my theory."

They were only eight hundred feet from the surface now.

Lucky said, "Good navigation, by the way. I mean the way you rammed the patch, Bigman."

"It's nothing," said Bigman, but he flushed with pleasure at the approval in Lucky's words.

He looked at the pressure dial. It was five hundred feet to the surface.

Silence fell.

And then there came a grating and scraping sound from overhead, a sudden interruption in their smooth climb, a laboring of their engines, and then a quick lightening of the view outside the porthole, together with an eye-blinking vision of cloudy sky and rolling water surface oozing up between shreds and fibers of weed. The water was pockmarked with tiny splashings.

"It's raining," said Lucky. "And now, I'm afraid, we'll have to sit tight and wait till the V-frogs come for us."

Bigman said blankly, "Well—well—— Here they are!"

For moving into view just outside the porthole, staring solemnly into the ship out of dark, liquid eyes, its long legs folded tightly down and its dexterous toes clasping a seaweed stem in a firm grip, was a V-frog!

Chapter 13

MINDS MEET

THE *Hlda* RODE HIGH in the tossing waters of the Venusian ocean. The splatter of strong, steady rain drummed its sound upon the outer hull in what was almost an Earthlike rhythm. To Bigman, with his Martian background, rain and ocean were alien, but to Lucky it brought memories of home.

Bigman said, "Look at the V-frog, Lucky. Look at it!"

"I see it," said Lucky calmly.

Bigman swept the glass with his sleeve and then found himself with his nose pressing against it for a better look.

Suddenly he thought, Hey, I better not get too close.

He sprang back, then deliberately put the little finger of each hand into the corners of his mouth and drew them apart. Sticking his tongue out, he crossed his eyes and wiggled his fingers.

The V-frog stared at him solemnly. It had not budged a muscle since it had first been sighted. It merely swayed solemnly with the wind. It did not seem to mind, or even to be aware of, the water that splashed about it and upon it.

Bigman contorted his face even more horribly and went "A-a-gh" at the creature.

Lucky's voice sounded over his shoulder. "What are you doing, Bigman?"

Bigman jumped, took his hands away, and let his face spring back into its own pixy-ish appearance. He said, grinning, "I was just showing that V-frog what I thought of it."

"And it was just showing you what it thought of you!"

Bigman's heart skipped a beat. He heard the clear disapproval in Lucky's voice. In such a crisis, at a time of such danger, he, Bigman, was making faces like a fool. Shame came over him.

He quavered, "I don't know what got into me, Lucky."

"*They* did," said Lucky, harshly. "Understand that. The V-frogs are feeling you out for weak points. However they can do it, they'll crawl into your mind, and once there they may remain past your ability to force them to leave. So don't follow any impulse until you've thought it out."

"Yes, Lucky," muttered Bigman.

"Now, what next?" Lucky looked about the ship. Evans was sleeping, tossing fitfully and breathing with difficulty. Lucky's eyes rested on him for a bare moment, then turned away.

Bigman said almost timidly, "Lucky?"

"Well."

"Aren't you going to call the space station?"

For a moment Lucky stared at his little partner without comprehension. Then slowly the lines between his eyes smoothed away and he whispered, "Great Galaxy! I'd forgotten. Bigman, I'd forgotten! I never once thought of it."

Bigman cocked a thumb over his shoulder, pointing at the port into which the V-frog was still owlishly gazing. "You mean, it——?"

"I mean *they*. Space, there may be thousands of them out there!"

Half in shame Bigman admitted to himself the nature of his own feelings; he was almost glad that Lucky had been trapped by the creatures as well as he. It relieved

him of some of the blame that might otherwise attach
to him. In fact, Lucky had no right——

Bigman stopped his thoughts, appalled. He was working himself into a resentment against Lucky. That
wasn't he. That was *they!*

Savagely he forced all thought from his mind and
concentrated on Lucky, whose fingers were now on the
transmitter, working them into the careful adjustment
required to reach finely out into space.

And then Bigman's head snapped back at a sudden
new and strange sound.

It was a voice, flat, without intonation. It said, "Do.
not tamper with your machine of far-reaching sound.
We do not wish it."

Bigman turned. His mouth fell open and, for a moment, stayed so. He said, "Who said that? Where is
it?"

Lucky said, "Easy, Bigman. It was inside your head."

"Not the V-frog!" said Bigman despairingly.

"Great Galaxy, what else can it be?"

And Bigman turned to stare out the port again, at the
clouds, the rain, and the swaying V-frog.

Once before in his life Lucky had felt the minds of
alien creatures impressing their thoughts upon him. That
had been on the day he had met the immaterial-energy
beings that dwelt within the hollow depths of Mars.
There his mind had been laid open, but the entry of
thought had been painless, even pleasant. He had known
his own helplessness, yet he had also been deprived of
all fear.

Now he faced something different. The mental fingers
inside his skull had forced their way in and he felt them
with pain, loathing, and resentment.

Lucky's hand had fallen away from the transmitter,
and he felt no urge to return to it. He had forgotten it
again.

The voice sounded a second time. "Make air vibra-
tions with your mouth."

Lucky said, "You mean, speak? Can you hear our thoughts when we do not speak?"

"Only very dimly and vaguely. It is very difficult unless we have studied your mind well. When you speak, your thoughts are sharper and we can hear."

"We hear you without trouble," said Lucky.

"Yes. We can send our thoughts powerfully and with strength. You cannot."

"Have you heard all I've said so far?"

"Yes."

"What do you wish of me?"

"In your thoughts we have detected an organization of your ellow beings far off, beyond the end, on the other side of the sky. You call it the Council. We wish to know more about it."

Inwardly Lucky felt a small spark of satisfaction. One question, at least, was answered. As long as he represented only himself, as an individual, the enemy was content to kill him. But in recent hours the enemy had discovered he had penetrated too much of the truth, and they were concerned about it.

Would other members of the Council learn as easily? What was the nature of this Council?

Lucky could understand the curiosity of the enemy, the new caution, the sudden desire to learn a little more from Lucky before killing him. No wonder the enemy had forborne forcing Evans to kill him even when the blaster was pointed and Lucky was helpless, forborne just an instant too long.

But Lucky buried further thought on the subject. They might, as they said, be unable to clearly hear unspoken thoughts. Then again, they might be lying.

He said abruptly, "What do you have against my people?"

The flat, emotionless voice said, "We cannot say what is not so."

Lucky's jaw hardened at that. Had they picked up his last thought concerning their lying? He would have to be careful, very careful.

The voice continued. "We do not think well of your

people. They end life. They eat meat. It is bad to be intelligent and to eat meat. One who eats meat must end life to live, and an intelligent meat eater does more harm than a mindless one since he can think of more ways to end life. You have little tubes that can end the lives of many at one time."

"But we do not kill V-frogs."

"You would if we let you. You even kill each other in large groups and small."

Lucky avoided comment on the last remark. He said, instead, "What is it you want of my people, then?"

"You grow numerous on Venus," said the voice. "You spread and take up room."

"We can take only so much," reasoned Lucky. "We can build cities only in the shallow waters. The deeps will always remain yours, and they form nine parts of the ocean's ten. Besides that, we can help you. If you have the knowledge of mind, we have the knowledge of matter. You have seen our cities and the machines of shining metal that go through air and water to worlds on the other side of the sky. With this power of ours, think how we can help you."

"There is nothing we need. We live and we think. We are not afraid and we do not hate. What more can we need? What should we do with your cities and your metal and your ships? How can it make life better for us?"

"Well, then, do you intend to kill us all?"

"We do not desire to end life. It is enough for us if we hold your minds so that we will know you will do no harm."

Lucky had a quick vision (his own? implanted?) of a race of men on Venus living and moving under the direction of the dominant natives, gradually being cut off from all connection with Earth, the generations growing more and more into complacent mental slaves.

He said, in words whose confidence he did not entirely feel, "Men cannot allow themselves to be controlled mentally."

"It is the only way, and you must help us."

"We will not."

"You have no choice. You must tell us of these lands beyond the sky, of the organization of your people, of what they will do against us, and how we may guard ourselves."

"There is no way you can make me do that."

"Is there not?" asked the voice. "Consider, then. If you will not speak the information we require, we will then ask you to descend back into the ocean in your machine of shining metal, and there at the bottom you will open your machine to the waters."

"And die?" said Lucky grimly.

"The end of your lives would be necessary. With your knowledge it would not be safe to allow you to mingle with your fellows. You might speak to them and cause them to attempt reprisals. That would not be good."

"Then I have nothing to lose by not telling you."

"You have much to lose. Should you refuse what we ask, we would have to delve into your mind by force. That is not efficient. We might miss much of value. To diminish that danger, we would have to take your mind apart bit by bit, and that would be unpleasant for you. It would be much better for us and for you if you were to help us freely."

"No." Lucky shook his head.

A pause. The voice began again: "Although your people are given to ending life, they fear having their own lives end. We will spare you that fear if you help us. When you descend into the ocean to your life's end, we will remove fear from your mind. If, however, you do not choose to help us, we will force you into life's end anyhow, but we will not remove fear. We will intensify it."

"No," said Lucky, more loudly.

Another pause, a longer one. Then the voice said, "We do not ask your knowledge out of fear for our own safety, but to make it unnecessary for ourselves to take measures of an unpleasant nature. If we are left with but uncertain knowledge as to how to guard ourselves against your people from the other side of the sky, then we will be forced to put an end to the threat by ending life for all your people on this world. We will let the ocean into their cities as we have already almost done to one of them. Life will end for your people like the quenching of a flame. It will be snuffed out, and life will burn no more."

Lucky laughed wildly. "Make me!" he said.

"Make you?"

"Make me speak. Make me dive the ship. Make me do *anything*."

"You think we cannot?"

"I know you cannot."

"Look about you, then, and see what we have already accomplished. Your fellow creature who is bound is in our hands. Your fellow creature who stood at your side is in our hands."

Lucky whirled. In all this time, through all this conversation, he had not heard Bigman's voice once. It was as though he had completely forgotten Bigman's existence. And now he saw the little Martian lying twisted and crumpled at his feet.

Lucky dropped to his knees, a vast and fearful dismay parching his throat. "You've killed him?"

"No, he lives. He is not even badly hurt. But, you see, you are alone now. You have none to help you now. They could not withstand us, and neither can you."

White-faced, Lucky said, "No. You will not make me do anything."

"One last chance. Make your choice. Do you choose to help us, so that life may end peacefully and quietly for you? Or will you refuse to help us, so that it must end in pain and sorrow, to be followed, perhaps, by life's end for all your people in the cities below the ocean? Which is it to be? Come, your answer!"

The words echoed and re-echoed within Lucky's mind as he prepared to stand, alone and unfriended, against the buffets of a mental power he did not know how to fight save by an unbending stubbornness of will.

Chapter 14

MINDS BATTLE

How DOES ONE SET UP A BARRIER against mental attack? Lucky had the desire to resist, but there were no muscles he could flex, no guard he could throw up, no way he could return violence. He must merely remain as he was, resisting all those impulses that flooded his mind which he could not surely tell to be his own.

And how could he tell which were his own? What did he himself wish to do? What did he *himself* wish most to do?

Nothing entered his mind. It was blank. Surely there *had* to be something. He had not come up here without a plan.

Up here?

Then he had come up. Originally, he had been down.

Far down in the recesses of his mind, he thought, Tha''s it.

He was in a ship. It had come up from the sea bottom. It was on the surface of the water now. Good. What next?

Why at the surface? Dimly he could remember it was safer underneath.

He bent his head with great difficulty, closed his eyes and opened them again. His thoughts were very thick.

He had to get word somewhere . . . somewhere . . . about something.

He had to get word.

Get word.

And he broke through! It was as though somewhere miles inside of himself he had put a straining shoulder to a door and it had burst open. There was a clear flash of purpose, and he remembered something he had forgotten.

Ship's radio and the space station, of course.

He said, huskily, "You haven't got me. Do you hear that? I remember, and I'll keep on remembering."

There was no answer.

He shouted aloud, incoherently. His mind was faintly occupied with the analogy of a man fighting an overdose of a sleeping drug. Keep the muscles active, he thought. Keep walking. Keep walking.

In his case, he had to keep his mind active, he had to keep the mental fibers working. Do something. Do something. Stop, and they'll get you.

He continued shouting, and sound became words, "I'll do it. I'll do it."

Do what? He could feel it slipping from him again.

Feverishly, he repeated to himself, "Radio to station . . . radio to station . . ." but the sounds were becoming meaningless.

He was moving now. His body turned clumsily as though his joints were wood and nailed in place, but it was turning. He faced the radio. He saw it clearly for a moment, then it wavered and became foggy. He bent his mind to the task, and it was clear again. He could see the transmitter, see the range-setting toggle and the frequency condensers. He could recall and understand its workings.

He took a dragging step toward it and a sensation as of red-hot spikes boring into his temples overwhelmed him.

He staggered and fell to his knees, then, in agony, rose again.

Through pain-hazed eyes, he could still make out the radio. First one of his legs moved, then another.

The radio seemed a hundred yards away, hazy, surrounded by a bloody mist. The pounding in Lucky's head increased with each step.

He fought to ignore the pain, to see only the radio, to think only of the radio. He forced his legs to move against a rubbery resistance that was entangling them and dragging him down.

Finally, he put out his arm, and when his fingers were still six inches away from the ultrawave, Lucky knew that his endurance was at an end. Try as he might, he could drive his exhausted body no closer. It was all over. It was ended.

The *Hilda* was a scene of paralysis. Evans lay unconscious on his cot; Bigman was crumpled on the floor; and though Lucky remained stubbornly upright, his trembling fingertips were the only sign of life in him.

The cold voice in Lucky's mind sounded once again in its even, inexorable monotone: "You are helpless, but you will not lose consciousness as did your companions. You will suffer this pain until you decide to submerge your ship, tell us what we wish to know, and end your life. We can wait patiently. There is no way you can resist us. There is no way you can fight us. No bribe! No threat!"

Lucky, through the endless torture, felt a striving within his sluggish, pain-soaked mind, the stirring of something new.

No bribe? No threat?

No bribe?

Even through the misty semiconsciousness, the spark in his mind caught fire.

He abandoned the radio, turned his thoughts away, and instantly the curtain of pain lifted a fraction. Lucky took a faltering step away from the radio, and it lifted a bit more. He turned away completely.

Lucky tried not to think. He tried to act automatically and without foreplanning. They were concentrating on preventing his reaching the radio. They must not realize the other danger they faced. The pitiless enemy must not deduce his intentions and try to stop him. He would have to act quickly. They must not stop him.

They *must* not!

He had reached the first-aid wall chest and flung open its door. He could not see clearly, and he lost precious seconds in fumbling.

The voice said, "What is your decision?" and the fierceness of pain began to clamp down upon the young councilman once more.

Lucky had it—a squat jar of bluish silicone. His fingers groped through what seemed deadening cotton for the little catch that would shut off the paramagnetic microfield that held the jar's lid closed and airtight.

He scarcely felt the little nudge as one fingernail caught the catch. He scarcely saw the lid move to one side and fall off. He scarcely heard it hit the floor with the sound of metastic against metal. Fuzzily, he could see that the jar was open, and hazily, he lifted his arm toward the trash ejector.

The pain had returned in all its fury.

His left arm had lifted the hinged opening of the ejector; his right arm tremblingly raised the precious jar to the six-inch opening.

His arm moved for an eternity. He could no longer see. A red haze covered everything.

He felt his arm and the jar it held strike the wall. He pushed, but it would move no farther. The fingers on his left hand inched down from where they held the opening of the trash ejector, and touched the jar.

He daren't drop it now. If he did, he would never in his life find the strength to pick it up again.

He had it in both hands, and together both hands pulled at it. It inched upward, while Lucky hovered closer and closer to the edge of unconsciousness.

And then the jar was gone!

A million miles away, it seemed, he could hear the whistle of compressed air, and he knew the jar had been ejected into the warm Venusian ocean.

For a moment the pain wavered and then, in one giant stroke, lifted completely.

Lucky righted himself carefully and stepped away from the wall. His face and body were drenched in perspiration, and his mind still reeled.

As fast as his still faltering steps could take him, he moved to the radio transmitter, and this time nothing stopped him.

Evans sat in a chair with his head buried in his arms. He had gulped thirstily at water and kept saying over and over again, "I don't remember a thing. I don't remember a thing."

Bigman, bare to the waist, was mopping at his head and chest with a damp cloth, and a shaky grin came to his face. "I do. I remember everything. One minute I was standing there listening to you talking to the voice, Lucky, and then with no warning I was flat on the floor. I couldn't feel a thing, I couldn't turn my head, I couldn't even blink my eyes, but I could hear everything that was going on. I could hear the voice and what you said, Lucky. I saw you start for the radio . . ."

He puffed his breath out and shook his head.

"I never made it that first time, you know," said Lucky quietly.

"I couldn't tell. You passed out of my field of vision, and after that all I could do was lie there and wait to hear you start sending. Nothing happened, and I kept thinking they must have you, too. In my mind, I could see all three of us lying in living death. It was all over, and I couldn't nudge a thumbnail. It was all I could do just to breathe. Then you moved back past my eyes again, and I wanted to laugh and cry and yell all at the same time, but all I could do was lie there. I could just about make you out, Lucky, clawing at the wall. I couldn't tell what on Venus you were doing, but a few minutes later it was all over. Wow!"

Evans said wearily, "And we're really heading back for Aphrodite now, Lucky? No mistake?"

"We're heading back unless the instruments are lying,

and I don't think they are," said Lucky. "When we do get back and we can spare the time, we'll all of us get a little medical attention."

"Sleep!" insisted Bigman. "That's all I want. Just two days of solid sleep."

"You'll get that, too," said Lucky.

But Evans, more than the other two, was haunted by the experience. It showed quite plainly in the way he huddled in his own arms and slouched, almost cowered, in his chair. He said, "Aren't they interfering with us in any way at all any more?" There was the lightest emphasis on the word *they*.

"I can't guarantee that," said Lucky, "but the worst of the affair is over in a way. I reached the space station."

"You're sure? There's no mistake?"

"None at all. They even relayed me to Earth and I spoke to Conway directly. That part is settled."

"Then it's *all* settled," crowed Bigman joyously. "Earth is prepared. It knows the truth about the V-frogs."

Lucky smiled, but offered no comment.

Bigman said, "Just one thing, Lucky. Tell me what happened. How did you break their hold? Sands of Mars! What did you do?"

Lucky said, "Nothing that I ought not to have thought of long in advance and saved us all a great deal of needless trouble. The voice told us that all they needed in life was to live and to think. You recall that, Bigman? It said later on that we had no way of threatening them and no way of bribing them? It was only at the last moment that I realized you and I knew better."

"*I* know better?" said Bigman blankly.

"Certainly you do. You found out two minutes after you saw your first V-frog, that life and thought is *not* all they need. I told you on the way to the surface that Venusian plants stored oxygen so that Venusian animals got their oxygen from their food and didn't have to breathe. In fact, I said, they probably get too much oxygen and that's why they're so fond of low-oxygen food like hydrocarbons. Like axle grease, for instance. Don't you remember?"

Bigman's eyes were widening. "Sure."

"Just think how they must crave hydrocarbon. It must be like the craving of a child for candy."

Bigman said once again, "Sure."

"Now the V-frogs had us under mental control, but to maintain us under such control, they had to concentrate. What I had to do was distract them, at least to distract those that were nearest the ship, and whose power over us was strongest. So I threw out the obvious thing."

"But what? Don't play cute, Lucky."

"I threw out an open jar of petroleum jelly, which I got out of the medicine cabinet. It's pure hydrocarbon, of much higher grade than the axle grease. They couldn't resist. Even with so much at stake, they couldn't resist. Those nearest to the jar dived for it. Others farther away were in mental rapport, and their minds turned instantly to hydrocarbon. They lost control of us, and I was able to put through the call. That was all."

"Well, then," said Evans, "we're through with them."

"If it comes to that," said Lucky, "I'm not at all certain. There are a few things——"

He turned away, frowning, his lips clamped shut, as though he had already spoken too much.

The dome glimmered gorgeously outside the port, and Bigman felt his heart lift at the sight. He had eaten, even napped a bit, and his ebullient spirits bubbled as ever now. Lou Evans had recovered considerably from his own despondency. Only Lucky had not lost his look of wariness.

Bigman said, "I tell you the V-frogs are demoralized, Lucky. Look here, we've come back through a hundred miles of ocean, nearly, and they haven't touched us once. Well, have they?"

Lucky said, "Right now, I'm wondering why we don't get an answer from the dome."

Evans frowned in his turn. "They shouldn't take this long."

Bigman looked from one to the other. "You don't think anything can be wrong inside the city, do you?"

Lucky waved his hand for silence. A voice came in over the receiver, low and rapid.

"Identification, please."

Lucky said, "This is the Council-chartered subship *Hilda*, out of Aphrodite, returning to Aphrodite. David Starr in charge and speaking."

"You will have to wait."

"For what reason, please?"

"The locks are all in operation in the moment."

Evans frowned and muttered, "That's impossible, Lucky."

Lucky said, "When will one be free? Give me its location, and direct me to its vicinity by ultrasignal."

"You will have to wait."

The connection remained open, but the man at the other end spoke no more.

Bigman said indignantly, "Get Councilman Morriss, Lucky. That'll get some action."

Evans said hesitantly, "Morriss thinks I'm a traitor. Do you suppose he could have decided that you've thrown in with me, Lucky?"

"If so," said Lucky, "he'd be anxious to get us into the city. No, it's my thought that the man we've been speaking to is under mental control."

Evans said, "To stop us from getting in? Are you serious?"

"I'm serious."

"There's no way they can stop us from getting in in the long run unless they——" Evans paled and moved to the porthole in two rapid strides. "Lucky, you're right! They're bringing a cannon blaster to bear! They're going to blow us out of the water!"

Bigman was at the porthole, too. There was no mistake about it. A section of the dome had moved to one side, and through it, somewhat unreal as seen through water, was a squat tube.

Bigman watched the muzzle lower and center upon them, with fascinated horror. The *Hilda* was unarmed. It could never gain velocity fast enough to escape being blasted. There seemed no way out of instant death.

Chapter 15

THE ENEMY?

BUT EVEN AS BIGMAN felt his stomach constrict at the prospect of imminent destruction, he could hear Lucky's even voice speaking forcefully into the transmitter:

"Subship *Hilda* arriving with cargo of petroleum . . . Subship *Hilda* arriving with cargo of petroleum . . . Subship *Hilda* arriving with cargo of petroleum . . . Subship *Hilda*——"

An agitated voice broke through from the other end. "Clement Heber at lock control at this end. What is wrong? Repeat. What is wrong? Clement Heber——"

Bigman yelled, "They're withdrawing the blaster, Lucky."

Lucky let out his breath in a puff, but only in that way did he show any sign of tension. He said into the transmitter, "Subship *Hilda* reporting for entrance to Aphrodite. Please assign lock. Repeat. Please assign lock."

"You may have lock number fifteen. Follow directional signal. There seems to be some confusion here."

Lucky rose and said to Evans, "Lou, take the controls and get the ship into the city as fast as you can." He motioned Bigman to follow him to the other room.

"What—what——" Bigman spluttered like a leaky popgun.

Lucky sighed and said, "I thought the V-frogs would

try to arrange to have us kept out, so I was all set with the petroleum trick. But I didn't think things would get so bad they would point a cannon at us. That made it really tough. I wasn't as sure as all that that the petroleum notion would work."

"But how did it?"

"Hydrocarbon again. Petroleum is hydrocarbon. My word came over the open radio and the V-frogs who had the dome guards under control were distracted."

"How come they knew what petroleum was?"

"I pictured it in my mind, Bigman, with every bit of imagination I had. They can read minds when you sharpen the mental pictures by speaking, you know.

"But never mind all that." His voice dropped to a whisper. "If they're ready to blow us out of the ocean, if they're ready for something as crudely violent as that, they're desperate; and we're desperate, too. We've got to bring this to an end right away, and we've got to do the right thing. One mistake at this stage could be fatal."

From his shirt pocket Lucky had unclipped a scriber, and he was writing rapidly on a piece of foil.

He held it out to Bigman. "That's what you're to do when I give the word."

Bigman's eyes widened, "But Lucky——"

"Sh! Don't refer to any of this in words."

Bigman nodded, "But are you sure you're right?"

"I hope so." Lucky's handsome face was drawn with anxiety. "Earth knows about the V-frogs now, so they'll never win over humanity; but they may still do damage here on Venus. We've got to prevent that somehow. Now do you understand what you're to do?"

"Yes."

"In that case . . ." Lucky rolled the foil together and kneaded it with his strong fingers. The pellet that remained he returned to his shirt pocket.

Lou Evans called out, "We're in the lock, Lucky. In five minutes we'll be in the city."

Lucky said, "Good. Get Morriss on the radio."

They were in Council headquarters in Aphrodite again, the same room, Bigman thought, in which he had first met Lou Evans; the same room in which he had first seen a V-frog. He shuddered at the thought of those mental tendrils infiltrating his mind for the first time without his knowledge.

That was the one way in which the room was different now. The aquarium was gone; the dishes of peas and of axle grease were gone; the tall tables stood bare at the false window.

Morriss had pointed that out mutely as soon as they entered. His plump cheeks sagged and the lines of strain about his eyes were marked. His pudgy handshake was uncertain.

Carefully Bigman put what he was carrying on top of one of the tables. "Petroleum jelly," he said.

Lou Evans sat down. So did Lucky.

Morriss did not. He said, "I got rid of the V-frogs in this building. That was all I could do. I can't ask people to do away with their pets without a reason. And I couldn't give the reason, obviously."

"It will be enough," said Lucky. "Throughout this discussion, though, I want you to keep your eyes on the hydrocarbon. Keep its existence firmly in your mind."

"You think that will help?" asked Morriss.

"I think it will."

Morriss stopped his pacing immediately before Lucky. His voice was a sudden bluster. "Starr, I can't believe this. The V-frogs have been in the city for years. They've been here almost since the city was built."

"You've got to remember——" began Lucky.

"That I'm under their influence?" Morriss reddened. "That isn't so. I deny it."

"There's nothing to be ashamed of, Dr. Morriss," said Lucky, crisply. "Evans was under their control for days, and Bigman and I have been controlled, too. It is possible to be honestly unaware that your mind has been continuously picked."

"There's no proof of it, but never mind," said Morriss

violently. "Suppose you're right. The question is, what can we do? How do we fight them? Sending men against them will be useless. If we bring in a fleet to bombard Venus from space, they may force the dome locks open and drown every city on Venus in revenge. We could never kill every V-frog on Venus anyway. There are eight hundred million cubic miles of ocean for them to hide in, and they can multiply fast if they want to. Now your getting word to Earth was essential, I admit, but it still leaves us with many important problems."

"You're right," admitted Lucky, "but the point is, I didn't tell Earth everything. I couldn't until I was certain I knew the truth. I——"

The intercom signal flashed, and Morriss barked. "What is it?"

"Lyman Turner for his appointment, sir," was the answer.

"One second." The Venusian turned to Lucky and said in a low voice, "Are you sure we want him?"

"You had this appointment about strengthening the transite partitions within the city, didn't you?"

"Yes, but——"

"And Turner is a victim. The evidence would seem to be clear there. He is the one highly-placed official beside ourselves who would definitely seem to be one. We would want to see him, I think."

Morriss said into the intercom, "Send him up."

Turner's gaunt face and hooked nose made up a mask of inquiry as he entered. The silence in the room and the way the others stared at him would have filled even a far less sensitive man with foreboding.

He swung his computer case to the floor and said, "Is anything wrong, gentlemen?"

Slowly, carefully, Lucky gave him the bare outline of the matter.

Turner's thin lips parted. He said, weakly, "You mean, *my* mind——"

"How else would the man at the lock have known the exact manner in which to keep out intruders? He was unskilled and untrained, yet he barricaded himself in with electronic perfection."

"I never thought of that. I never thought of that." Turner's voice was almost an incoherent mumble. How could I have missed it?"

"They wanted you to miss it," said Lucky.

"It makes me ashamed."

"You have company in that, Turner. Myself, Dr. Morriss, Councilman Evans——"

"Then what do we do about it?"

Lucky said, "Exactly what Dr. Morriss was asking when you arrived. It will need all our thought. One of the reasons I suggested you be brought into this gathering is that we may require your computer."

"Oceans of Venus, I hope so," said Turner fervently. "If I could do something to make up for——" And he put his hand to his forehead as though half in fear that he had a strange head on his shoulders, one not his own.

He said, "Are we ourselves now?"

Evans put in, "We will be as long as we concentrate on that petroleum jelly."

"I don't get it. Why should that help?"

"It does. Never mind how for the moment," said Lucky. "I want to get on with what I was about to say when you arrived."

Bigman swung back to the wall and perched himself on the table where the aquarium once stood. He stared idly at the open jar on the other table as he listened.

Lucky said, "Are we sure the V-frogs are the real menace?"

"Why, that's your theory," said Morriss with surprise.

"Oh, they're the immediate means of controlling the minds of mankind, granted; but are they the real enemy? They're pitting their minds against the minds of Earthmen and proving formidable opponents, yet individual V-frogs seem quite unintelligent."

"How so?"

"Well, the V-frog you had in this place did not have the good sense to keep out of our minds. He broadcast his surprise at our being without mustaches. He ordered Bigman to get him peas dipped in axle grease. Was that intelligent? He gave himself away immediately."

Morriss shrugged. "Maybe not all V-frogs are intelligent."

"It goes deeper than that. We were helpless in their mental grip out on the ocean surface. Still, because I guessed certain things, I tried a jar of petroleum jelly on them, and it worked. It scattered them. Mind you, their entire campaign was at stake. They had to keep us from informing Earth concerning them. Yet they ruined everything for one jar of petroleum jelly. Again, they almost had us when we were trying to re-enter Aphrodite. The cannon was coming to an aim when the mere mention of petroleum spoiled their plans."

Turner stirred in his seat. "I understand what you mean by the petroleum now, Starr. Everyone knows the V-frogs have a craving for grease of all sorts. The craving is just too strong for them."

"Too strong for beings sufficiently intelligent to battle Earthmen? Would you abandon a vital victory, Turner, for a steak or a wedge of chocolate cake?"

"Of course I wouldn't, but that doesn't prove a V-frog wouldn't."

"It doesn't, I grant you. The V-frog mind is alien to us and we can't suppose that what works with us must work with them. Still, the matter of their being diverted by hydrocarbon is suspicious. It makes me compare V-frogs with dogs rather than with men."

"In what way?" demanded Morriss.

"Think about it," said Lucky. "A dog can be trained to do many seemingly intelligent things. A creature who had never seen or heard of a dog before, watching a seeing-eye dog guide a blind master in the days before Son-O-Taps, would have wondered whether the dog or the man was the more intelligent. But if he passed by them with a meaty bone and noted that the dog's attention was instantly diverted, he would suspect the truth."

Turner said, his pale eyes nearly bulging, "Are you

trying to say that V-frogs are just the tools of human beings?"

"Doesn't that sound probable, Turner? As Dr. Morriss said just a while ago the V-frogs have been in the city for years, but it's only a matter of the last few months that they've been making trouble. And then the trouble started with trivialities, like a man giving away money in the streets. It is almost as though some men learned how to use the V-frogs' natural capacity for telepathy as tools with which to inflict their thoughts and orders on human minds. It is as though they had to practice at first, learn the nature and limitations of their tools, develop their control, until the time came when they could do big things. Eventually, it would be not the yeast that they were after but something more; perhaps control of the Solar Confederation, even of the entire galaxy."

"I can't believe it," said Morriss.

"Then I'll give you another piece of evidence. When we were out in the ocean, a mental voice—presumably that of a V-frog—spoke to us. It tried to force us to give it some information and then commit suicide."

"Well?"

"The voice arrived via a V-frog, but it did not originate with one. It originated with a human being."

Lou Evans sat bolt upright and stared incredulously at Lucky.

Lucky smiled. "Even Lou doesn't believe that, but it's so. The voice made use of odd concepts such as 'machines of shining metal' instead of 'ships.' We were supposed to think that V-frogs were unfamiliar with such concepts, and the voice had to stimulate our minds into imagining we heard round-about expressions that meant the same thing. But then the voice forgot itself. I remember what I heard it say. I remember it word for word: 'Life will end for your people like the quenching of a flame. It will be snuffed out and life will burn no more.' "

Morriss stolidly said again, "Well?"

"You still don't see it? How could the V-frogs use a

concept like the 'quenching of a flame' or 'life will burn no more'? If the voice pretends to be that of a V-frog with no concept of such a thing as a ship, how could it have one of fire?"

They all saw it, now, but Lucky drove on furiously. "The atmosphere of Venus is nitrogen and carbon dioxide. There is no oxygen. We all know that. Nothing can burn in Venus's atmosphere. There can be no flame. In a million years no V-frog could possibly have seen a fire, and none of them can know what it is. Even granted that some might have seen fire and flame within the city domes, they could have no understanding of its nature any more than they understood our ships. As I see it, the thoughts we received originated with no V-frog, but with a man who used the V-frog only as a channel to reach from his own mind to ours."

"But how could that be done?" asked Turner.

"I don't know," said Lucky. "I wish I did. Certainly it would take a brilliant mind to find a way. A man would have to know a great deal about the workings of a nervous system and about the electrical phenomena associated with it." Lucky looked coldly at Morriss. "It might take, for instance, a man who specialized in biophysics."

And all eyes turned on the Venusian councilman, from whose round face the blood was draining until his grizzled mustache seemed scarcely visible against his pale skin.

Chapter 16

THE ENEMY!

MORRISS MANAGED TO SAY, "Are you trying to——" and his voice ground hoarsely to a halt.

"I'm not making any definite statement," said Lucky smoothly. "I have merely made a suggestion."

Morriss looked helplessly about, turning from face to face of the four other men in the room, watching each pair of eyes meet his in fixed fascination.

He choked out, "This is mad, absolutely insane. I was the first to report all this—this—trouble on Venus. Find the original report in Council headquarters. My name is on it. Why should I call in the Council if I were—— And my motive? Eh? My motive?"

Councilman Evans seemed uneasy. From the quick glance he shot in Turner's direction, Bigman guessed that this form of inter-Council squabble in front of an outsider was not to his liking.

Still, Evans said, "It would explain the effort Dr. Morriss made to discredit me. I was an outsider, and I might stumble on the truth. I had found half of it, certainly."

Morriss was breathing heavily. "I deny that I ever did such a thing. All this is a conspiracy of some sort against me, and it will go hard in the end for any of you who join in this. I will have justice."

"Are you implying that you wish a Council trial?"

asked Lucky. "Do you want to plead your case before a meeting of the assembled Central Committee of the Council?"

What Lucky was referring to, of course, was the procedure ordained for the trial of councilmen accused of high treason against the Council and the Solar Confederation. In all the history of the Council, not one man had ever had to stand such a trial.

At its mention, whatever shreds of control Morriss had used to restrain his feelings vanished. Roaring, he scrambled to his feet and hurtled blindly at Lucky.

Lucky rolled nimbly up and over the arm of the chair he occupied and, at the same time, gestured quickly at Bigman.

It was the signal that Bigman was waiting for. Bigman proceeded to follow the instructions Lucky had given him on board the *Hilda* when they were passing through the lock of Aphrodite's dome.

A blaster bolt shot out. It was at low intensity but its ionizing radiations produced the pungent odor of ozone in the air.

Matters remained so for a moment. All motion ceased. Morriss, his head against the overturned chair, made no move to get up. Bigman remained standing, like a small statue, with his blaster still held against his hip as though he had been frozen in the act of shooting.

And the target of the blaster bolt lay destroyed and in ruins upon the floor.

Lou Evans found his breath first, but it was only for a sharp exclamation, "What in space———"

Lyman Turner whispered, "What have you done?"

Morriss, panting from his recent effort, could say nothing, but he rolled his eyes mutely at Bigman.

Lucky said, "Nice shot, Bigman," and Bigman grinned.

And in a hundred fragments Lyman Turner's black computer case lay smashed and, for the most part, disintegrated.

Turner's voice rose. "My computer! You *idiot!* What have you done?"

Lucky said sternly, "Only what he had to do, Turner. Now, everyone quiet."

He turned to Morriss, helped that plump personage to his feet, and said, "All my apologies, Dr. Morriss, but I had to make certain that Turner's attention was completely misdirected. I had to use you for that purpose."

Morriss said, "You mean you *don't* suspect me of—of——"

"Not for one minute," said Lucky. "I never did."

Morriss moved away, his eyes hot and angry, "Then suppose you explain, Starr."

Lucky said, "Before this conference, I never dared tell anyone that I thought some man was behind the V-frogs. I couldn't even state it in my message to Earth. It seemed obvious to me that if I were to do so, the real enemy might be desperate enough to take some action—such as actually flooding one of the cities—and hold the possibility of a repetition over the heads of all of us as blackmail. As long as he did not know that I went past the V-frog in my suspicions, I hoped he would hold off and play for time or, at most, try to kill only my friends and myself.

"At this conference I could speak of the matter because I believed the man in question to be present. However, I dared not take action against him without proper preparation for fear that he might place us under control despite the presence of the petroleum and for fear that his actions thereafter would be drastic. First I had to distract his attention thoroughly to make sure that, for a few seconds at least, he would be too absorbed in the surface activities of the group to detect, via his V-frog tools, the strong emotions that might be leaking out of Bigman's mind and mine. To be sure, there are no V-frogs in the building, but he might well be able to use the V-frogs in other parts of the city as he was able to use V-frogs out on the ocean's surface miles away from Aphrodite.

"To distract him then, I accused you, Dr. Morriss. I couldn't warn you in advance because I wanted your emotions to be authentic—and they were admirably so. Your attack on me was all that was needed."

Morriss withdrew a large handkerchief from a sleeve pocket and mopped his glistening forehead. "That was pretty drastic, Lucky, but I think I understand. Turner is the man, then?"

"He is," said Lucky.

Turner was on his knees, scrabbling among the fused and shattered shards of his instrument. He looked up with hate-filled eyes, "You've destroyed my computer."

"I doubt that it was a computer," said Lucky. "It was too inseparable a companion of yours. When I first met you, you had it with you. You stated you were using it to compute the strength of the inner barriers of the city against the threatened flood. Right now you have it with you presumably to help you if you should require new computations for your discussions with Dr. Morriss on the strength of those same inner barriers."

Lucky paused, then went on with a hard calmness in his voice. "But I came to see you in your apartment the morning after the threatened flood. I was merely planning to ask you some questions that involved no computing and you knew that. Yet you had your computer with you. You could not bring yourself to leave it in the next room. It had to be with you, at your feet. Why?"

Turner said desperately. "It was my own construction. I was fond of it. I always carried it with me."

"I should judge it weighed some twenty-five pounds. Rather heavy, even for affection. Could it be that it was the device you used to maintain touch with the V-frogs at all times?"

"How do you intend to prove that?" flashed back Turner. "You said I myself was a victim. Everyone here is witness to that."

"Yes," said Lucky, "the man who, despite inexperience, so expertly barricaded himself at the dome lock, got his information from you. But was that information stolen from your mind or did you yourself donate it freely?"

Morriss said angrily, "Let me put the question directly, Lucky. Are you or are you not responsible for the epidemic of mental control, Turner?"

"Of course I'm not," cried Turner. "You can't do anything just on the say-so of a young fool who thinks he can make guesses and have them stick because he's on the Council."

Lucky said, "Tell me, Turner, do you remember that night when a man sat at one of the dome locks with a lever in his hand? Do you remember it well?"

"Quite well."

"Do you remember coming to me and telling me that if the locks were opened the inner transite barrier would not hold and that all of Aphrodite would be flooded? You were quite frightened. Almost panicky."

"All right. I was. I still am. It's something to be panicky about." He added, with his lip curling, "Unless you're the brave Lucky Starr."

Lucky ignored that. "Did you come to me with that information in order to add a little to the already existing confusion, to make sure that we were all disconcerted long enough for you to maneuver Lou Evans out of the city in order that he might be safely killed in the ocean? Evans was hard to handle, and he had learned too much concerning the V-frogs. Perhaps, also, you were trying to frighten me out of Aphrodite and off Venus."

Turner said, "This is all ridiculous. The inner barriers *are* inadequate. Ask Morriss. He's already seen my figures."

Morriss noded reluctantly. "I'm afraid Turner is right there."

"No matter," said Lucky. "Let's consider that settled. There was a real danger, and Turner was justifiably panicked. . . . You are married, Turner."

Turner's eyes flicked uneasily to Lucky's face and away again. "So?"

"Your wife is pretty and considerably younger than yourself. You have been married for not quite a year."

"What is that intended to prove?"

"That you probably have a deep affection for her. Immediately after marriage you move into an expensive apartment to please her; you allow her to decorate it according to her tastes even though your own taste differs. Surely you wouldn't neglect her safety, would you?"

"I don't understand. What are you talking about?"

"I think you know. The one time I met your wife she told me that she had slept through the entire excitement the night before. She seemed quite disappointed that she had. She also told me what a fine apartment house she lived in. She said it even possessed 'chambers.' Unfortunately, that meant nothing to me at the time, or I might have seen the truth then and there. It was only later, at the bottom of the ocean, that Lou Evans casually mentioned chambers and told me what they were. 'Chambers' is a word used on Venus to denote special shelters built to withstand the full force of the ocean in case a quake breaks a city dome. Now do you know what I'm talking about?"

Turner was silent.

Lucky went on. "If you were so frightened of city-wide catastrophe that night, why didn't you think of your wife? You spoke of rescuing people, of escaping the city. Did you never consider your wife's safety? There were chambers in the basement of her apartment house. Two minutes and she would have been safe. You had only to call her, give her one word of warning. But you didn't. You let her sleep."

Turner mumbled something.

Lucky said, "Don't say you forgot. That's completely unbelievable. You might have forgotten anything, but not your wife's safety. Let me suggest an alternative explanation. You were not worried about your wife because you knew she was in no real danger. You knew she was in no real danger because you knew the lock in the dome would never be opened." Lucky's

voice was hard with anger. "You knew the lock in the
dome would never be opened because you yourself were
in mental control of the man at the lever. It was your
very fondness for your wife that betrayed you. You
could not bring yourself to disturb her sleep merely in
order to make your phony act more plausible."

Turner said suddenly, "I'm not saying anything more
without a lawyer. What you have isn't evidence."

Lucky said, "It's enough to warrant a full Council
investigation, though. . . . Dr. Morriss, would you have
him taken in custody in preparation for flight under
guard to Earth? Bigman and I will go with him. We'll
see that he gets there safely."

At the hotel again, Bigman said worriedly, "Sands
of Mars, Lucky, I don't see how we're going to get
proof against Turner. All your deductions sound con-
vincing and all that, but it isn't legal proof."

Lucky, with a warm yeast dinner inside himself, was
able to relax for the first time since he and Bigman had
penetrated the cloud barrier that encircles Venus. He
said, "I don't think the Council will be mainly interested
in legal proof or in getting Turner executed."

"Lucky! Why not? That cobber——"

"I know. He's a murderer several times over. He
definitely had dictatorial ambitions, so he's a traitor,
too. But more important than either of those things is
the fact that he created a work of genius."

Bigman said, "You mean his machine?"

"I certainly do. We destroyed the only one in existence, probably, and we'll need him to build another.
There are many questions we'd like answered. How did
Turner control the V-frogs? When he wanted Lou
Evans killed, did he instruct the V-frogs in detail, tell
them every step of the procedure, order them to bring
up the giant patch? Or did he simply say, 'Kill Evans,'
and allow the V-frogs to do their jobs like trained dogs
in whatever way they thought best?

"Then, too, can you imagine the use to which an instrument such as that can be put? It may offer us an

entirely new method of attack on mental diseases, a new way of combating criminal impulses. It may even, conceivably, be used to prevent wars in the future or to defeat the enemies of Earth quickly and bloodlessly if a war is forced upon us. Just as the machine was dangerous in the hands of one ambition-riddled man, it can be very useful and beneficial in the hands of the Council."

Bigman said, "Do you think the Council will argue him into building another machine?"

"I think so, and with proper safeguards, too. If we offer him pardon and rehabilitation, with an alternative of life imprisonment with no chance of ever seeing his wife again, I think he'll agree to help. And, of course, one of the first uses of the machine would be to investigate Turner's own mind, help cure it of his abnormal desire for power, and save for the service of humanity a first-class brain."

The next day they would be leaving Venus, heading once again for Earth. Lucky thought with pleasant nostalgia of the beautiful blue sky of his home planet, the open air, the natural foods, the space and scope of land life. He said, "Remember, Bigman, it is easy to 'protect society' by executing a criminal, but that will not bring back his victims. If one can cure him instead and use him to make life better and brighter for that society, how much more has been accomplished!"

NEL BESTSELLERS

Crime

T012 484	FIVE RED HERRINGS	*Dorothy L. Sayers*	40p
T015 556	MURDER MUST ADVERTISE	*Dorothy L. Sayers*	40p
T014 398	STRIDING FOLLY	*Dorothy L. Sayers*	30p

Fiction

T015 386	THE NORTHERN LIGHT	*A. J. Cronin*	50p
T016 544	THE CITADEL	*A. J. Cronin*	75p
T015 130	THE MONEY MAKER	*John J. McNamara Jr.*	50p
T013 820	THE DREAM MERCHANTS	*Harold Robbins*	75p
T018 105	THE CARPETBAGGERS	*Harold Robbins*	95p
T016 560	WHERE LOVE HAS GONE	*Harold Robbins*	75p
T013 707	THE ADVENTURERS	*Harold Robbins*	80p
T006 743	THE INHERITORS	*Harold Robbins*	60p
T009 467	STILETTO	*Harold Robbins*	30p
T015 289	NEVER LEAVE ME	*Harold Robbins*	40p
T016 579	NEVER LOVE A STRANGER	*Harold Robbins*	75p
T011 798	A STONE FOR DANNY FISHER	*Harold Robbins*	60p
T015 874	79 PARK AVENUE	*Harold Robbins*	60p
T011 461	THE BETSY	*Harold Robbins*	75p
T013 340	SUMMER OF THE RED WOLF	*Morris West*	50p

Historical

T013 758	THE LADY FOR RANSOM	*Alfred Duggan*	40p
T015 297	COUNT BOHEMOND	*Alfred Duggan*	50p
T010 279	MASK OF APOLLO	*Mary Renault*	50p
T014 045	TREASURE OF PLEASANT VALLEY	*Frank Yerby*	35p
T015 602	GILLIAN	*Frank Yerby*	50p

Science Fiction

T015 017	EQUATOR	*Brian Aldiss*	30p
T014 347	SPACE RANGER	*Isaac Asimov*	30p
T015 491	PIRATES OF THE ASTEROIDS	*Isaac Asimov*	30p
T016 331	THE CHESSMEN OF MARS	*Edgar Rice Burroughs*	40p
T013 537	WIZARD OF VENUS	*Edgar Rice Burroughs*	30p
T009 696	GLORY ROAD	*Robert Heinlein*	40p
T016 900	STRANGER IN A STRANGE LAND	*Robert Heinlein*	75p
T011 844	DUNE	*Frank Herbert*	75p
T012 298	DUNE MESSIAH	*Frank Herbert*	40p
T015 211	THE GREEN BRAIN	*Frank Herbert*	30p

War

T013 367	DEVIL'S GUARD	*Robert Elford*	50p
T015 505	THE LAST VOYAGE OF GRAF SPEE	*Michael Powell*	30p
T015 661	JACKALS OF THE REICH	*Ronald Seth*	30p
T012 263	FLEET WITHOUT A FRIEND	*John Vader*	30p

Western

T016 994	No. 1 EDGE – THE LONER	*George G. Gilman*	30p
T016 536	No. 5 EDGE – BLOOD ON SILVER	*George G. Gilman*	30p
T017 621	No. 6 EDGE – THE BLUE, THE GREY AND THE RED		
		George G. Gilman	30p
T014 479	No. 7 EDGE – CALIFORNIA KILLING	*George G. Gilman*	30p
T015 254	No. 8 EDGE – SEVEN OUT OF HELL	*George G. Gilman*	30p
T015 475	No. 9 EDGE – BLOODY SUMMER	*George G. Gilman*	30p

General

T011 763	SEX MANNERS FOR MEN	*Robert Chartham*	30p
W002 531	SEX MANNERS FOR ADVANCED LOVERS	*Robert Chartham*	25p
W002 835	SEX AND THE OVER FORTIES	*Robert Chartham*	30p
T010 732	THE SENSUOUS COUPLE	*Dr. 'C'*	25p

NEL P.O. BOX 11, FALMOUTH, TR10 9EN, CORNWALL
  Please send cheque or postal order. Allow 10p to cover postage and packing on one book plus 4p for each additional book.

Name ....

Address..

....

Title ....
(SEPTEMBER)